W9-CKF-913

She Never Dreamed
A Kiss Could Be Like This

She looked up at him, hardly seeing him through her tears. She had neither the will nor the ability to move away. He took his hand from hers and put it on her shoulder, turning her to face him, and then she was pulled against him and his arms were about her so tightly that she could hardly breathe, her face pressed into the thick, soft material of his jacket front. She could feel the urgency in his hard, powerful grasp, the tautness of his body. He took a crisp white handkerchief from his top pocket and gently wiped away the remaining tears from her cheeks; almost without thought she smiled tremulously.

As though the smile released him Luke tipped her chin up and kissed her softly on the lips. Anne's hands slid up over the lapels of his jacket and lightly her fingers touched the hair at the back of his neck. He felt the movement and stiffened, and then once more she was dragged against him, the kiss deepening, her mouth opening beneath his. In all her wildest imaginings Anne had never dreamed a kiss could be thus; filled with delight she clung round his neck, her eyes tightly closed as she seemed to drown with sensation.

Bantam Circle of Love Romances
Ask your bookseller for the books you have missed

Dear Friend,

Enter the Circle of Love—and travel to faraway places with romantic heroes . . .

We read hundreds of novels and, each month, select the very best—from the finest writers around the world—to bring you these wonderful love stories . . . that let *you* share in a variety of beautiful romantic experiences.

With Circle of Love Romances, you treat yourself to a romantic holiday—anytime, anywhere. And because we want to please you, won't you write and let us know your comments and suggestions?

Meanwhile, welcome to the Circle of Love—we don't think you'll ever want to leave!

Best,

Cathy Camhy
Editor

CIRCLE OF LOVE

Gold In Her Hair

Anne Neville

BANTAM BOOKS
TORONTO · NEW YORK · LONDON · SYDNEY

GOLD IN HER HAIR

*A Bantam Book/published by arrangement with
Robert Hale, Ltd.*

PRINTING HISTORY
First published in Great Britain 1977

*CIRCLE OF LOVE, the garland and the ring designs are
trademarks of Bantam Books, Inc.*

Bantam edition/April 1982

All rights reserved.
Copyright © 1977 by Anne Neville.
Cover art copyright © 1982 by Bantam Books, Inc.
This book may not be reproduced in whole or in part, by
mimeograph or any other means, without permission.
For information address: Bantam Books, Inc.

ISBN 0-553-21502-7

Published simultaneously in the United States and Canada

Bantam Books are published by Bantam Books, Inc. Its
trademark, consisting of the words "Bantam Books" and the
portrayal of a rooster, is Registered in U.S. Patent and Trademark Office and in other countries. Marca Registrada. Bantam Books, Inc., 666 Fifth Avenue, New York, New York 10103.

PRINTED IN THE UNITED STATES OF AMERICA

0 9 8 7 6 5 4 3 2 1

One

There were four flights of stairs leading to the attic bed-sitter in which Anne lived and by the time he had climbed them all George Markham was beginning to feel every one of his seventy-two years. Outside the attic door he halted a moment to get his breath. He noticed that the door was open, so instead of knocking on it he gave it a push and called out, "Can I come in?"

Anne rushed out of the tiny kitchen area, concern on her face. "Grandad, you know you shouldn't try to climb all those stairs. For heaven's sake, sit down and get your breath back. Here." She removed a pile of freshly laundered "undies" from the one and only easy chair and helped him into it. "Sorry the room's in a bit of a mess."

"Mess" was the operative word, as every spare inch of space seemed to have at least one article of clothing draped across it. The room was large and airy; the ceiling on one side sloped away under the roof and there was a skylight as well as the attic window. Anne had done a lot of work turning what had once been a dull brown, dingy room into something habitable. She had painted the walls daffodil yellow and the woodwork white so that the overall effect was bright and spring-like. Anne, wearing a green jersey top and green corded slacks looked, her grandfather thought colorfully, like a chrysanthemum with that copper knob of hers.

"So you're really going through with it," George said, when his heart-beat had slowed to normal.

"Of course I am. I've got the plane tickets." She smiled quickly. "Would you like some tea? I've just made a fresh pot."

"I'd rather have something stronger," he grunted.

"I think I have a drop of scotch somewhere, left over from a party." She rummaged about among the mess of painting equipment stacked in one corner and emerged triumphant with a bottle of Teacher's. "Just enough for one. Here you are. Cheers, Grandad."

"Cheers, love. Ah, that's better."

"I'll go on with my packing if you don't mind." Her suitcase was open on the floor and half-filled, and now she knelt by it and began putting in some of the clothes scattered about her. "It's an awkward time of the year to go abroad," she said as she worked. "I've been told that Rome can be deadly cold or almost as hot as summer."

"So I suppose you'll just take the usual jeans and jumpers," he said, smiling fondly at her. "That's all you ever seem to wear. I sometimes wonder if the modern girl has legs. The young men of today miss a lot I must say. When I think of the joy we used to get from the occasional glimpse of a nice ankle. . . ."

"Oh, Grandad, you're incorrigible!" Anne laughed. "And you're also wrong about me. I've decided to change my image. I woke up last birthday realizing that I was twenty-four years old and still wearing the same kind of gear I wore when I was seventeen. I don't intend to become an eternal teenager. So I've gone all feminine. I'm taking dresses, and skirts and blouses, and only one pair of jeans. Okay?"

"Okay." They smiled happily at each other but Anne sensed the worry behind his smile. She knelt up and touched the old man's arm. He had been the mainstay of her life for so long that it was difficult to believe that he was getting old, that there would be a day when he would no longer be there as an ear for her problems, moral support and a constant source of good advice. "I'll be all right, you know. I mean, I've been abroad before."

"On school trips and with your family. This is different."

"I know, but after all, Rome is perfectly civilized and nothing awful is likely to happen. Grandad, you must see that I have to find out about Laura. I've thought and thought about this, purposely waiting until I have the time to—well, to take my time. I needn't rush into anything. I have four weeks if necessary, and you know I haven't gone into it lightly."

"Laura was highstrung," he commented. "She

reminded me of your grandmother's sister, Emma. Poor daft Emm she was always called, even when we were at school. Not that she was daft really, but she imagined things—she thought she had second sight and all that. Laura used to imagine things."

"I don't think she imagined what she wrote in that letter, and even if she did, well, I have to find out for my own peace of mind." Anne folded up the one long dress she was taking, a straight affair in old gold jersey silk, and smoothed her hands over the soft material. "Besides," she slowly added, "there's Lucy. . . ."

"Now look here, you're not thinking of all that nonsense your mother's always on about, I hope!" he said, so sharply that Anne looked up astonished. "Oh, that mother of yours! She's nearly as crazy as poor daft Emm, even if they weren't related in any way. Oh, I know she has more reason to behave strangely, poor soul, but it's time she got over it. That child belongs with her father. He's a rich man who can give her a good life. I know we don't know anything about him but that's no matter. Don't you start. . . ."

"Grandad!" Anne interrupted. "Do you honestly think I'm going to Rome purposely to snatch Lucy away and bring her back to England? I'm not that stupid. I've always argued with mother that the idea is ridiculous. I don't blame Luke Patterson for writing such stinking letters to mother about it. She has no right to custody of the child. No right legally or morally. But I do want to see Lucy. She's my

4

niece, the only one I'll ever have. She's four years old and all we have is a photograph." She smiled winningly. "Listen, I've saved up for years for this, so that I can fly to Rome and stay there, not with a holiday company but on my own. I would have gone eventually anyway, just to see Lucy, but now that this letter has come I must go and find out about it."

"Very well," he agreed. "I suppose you're right. Come to that, I'd like to see Lucy too. She's my great granddaughter, you know."

"I do know." Anne's green eyes flashed. "And no matter what you say, I think Luke Patterson ought to be shot for not spending a little of his wealth bringing her over to see her family. What's more, I shall jolly well tell him so when I see him!"

George Markham chuckled. She probably would, too. She didn't have that red hair for nothing!

Anne went on her own to Gatwick, resisting the various attempts of her family to accompany her. She wanted to hear no more of her mother's crazy ideas about abducting Lucy, or her grandfather's "Job's comforter" remarks. This, she reflected, as she bought a cup of coffee and sat to wait out the hour before boarding-time, was to be the great adventure of her life and she intended to enjoy every minute of it! She loved to be alone. Always a solitary person, almost an only child because Laura had been so much older, she was in no way scared of her own company. Nothing gave her greater pleasure than to be alone, enjoying the freedom of doing as she wished when she wished. Now she had a round-trip ticket to Ciampino airport, Rome, and money hard saved over three years, enough for her to stay in a cheapish hotel for anything up to four weeks. Four weeks in Rome! The thought of it twisted her inside with excitement and caused her long, slender artist's fingers to twitch. She had been once before, a two day stopover on the way to Sorrento with her family. Two days that gave brief, mouth-watering glimpses of visions of wonder that had remained indelibly printed upon her brain. But oh, to pause and really look at these wonders! To stand in Saint Peter's Square and sketch that statue of Saint Peter, her favorite saint; to draw the massive statues of the Heavenly Twins, Castor and Pollux, her own birth sign, who guarded the Capitoline Hill; to wander round the Vatican palace and to gaze at the ceiling of the Sistine Chapel . . . Anne was almost sick with delight at the thought of these and other treasures that were even now just a few hours from her reach.

She came out of her daydream, blinking, to realize that someone was speaking to her. A voice was insistently saying, "Excuse me."

"Yes?"

"It's just that I noticed the luggage label on your vanity case said Rome and they called the Rome flight a couple of minutes ago."

"Did they?" Hastily she clambered to her feet, gathering up vanity case, handbag, newspaper and raincoat—it had been raining when she left home—and smiled gratefully at the man who had spoken to her. He looked about her own age, a tall, thin man with dark crinkly hair and dark crinkly eyes. Now she came to think of it, he had been sitting at the table when she sat down.

"It's not always easy to hear things over the loudspeaker," he said.

"No, but actually I was daydreaming." They walked together to passport control. "Are you going to Rome?" Anne asked.

"Yes. Tom Edwards is the name."

"I'm Anne Markham." She handed over her passport to be inspected and then moved on towards the departure lounge. Tom Edwards joined her. "I'm going on holiday," he told her. "It's a rotten time to be going away, in early March, but the only time I could get away. If I don't go now, I don't expect I'll ever go."

"Me too," Anne said. "It's cheaper anyway. With Easter so late this year I reckon on a good four weeks before the crowds start arriving and push the prices up."

Anne had been hoping to be alone on the trip so that she could enjoy the journey but it looked as though Tom Edwards intended sticking. He clung to her side tenaciously as they crossed the tarmac to the I-11 super-jet that awaited them, and without any bother at all contrived to swap seats with the elderly lady who should have been sitting beside Anne. He gave Anne a cheeky grin as he sank down beside her and did up his seat belt. Philosophically, she decided to make the best of it. After all, there wouldn't be anything to look at; it wouldn't be the same as a train journey which she really loved. So she returned Tom's grin with a wide smile and he beamed at her. He could scarcely believe his luck in landing himself with such a travelling companion. Being the sort of young man who tended to fall heavily for the flashy, sophisticated sort—not that he met many of them!—he wouldn't say she was beautiful, but her eyes were a rare green and intelligent, her mouth when she smiled curved invitingly, and that red hair, straight and thick and falling to below her shoulders, was out of this world.

"Do you smoke?" he asked when they were airborne.

"I do occasionally. Yes, I think I will, please." Anne leaned forward so that he could light her cigarette. "Tell me, Tom, what sort of job do you do that they won't let you have a holiday except in March?"

"Oh, I'm a reporter," he said airily, with the sort of casual aplomb that told Anne he was really quite new to the job and proud as punch of it. She hid a smile and made admiring noises.

"That sounds exciting. Who do you work for?"

"I'm free-lancing now. I started on the local rag and worked my way up." He came down to earth for a moment, adding, "I seemed to spend my whole time covering weddings and the amateur operatic society 'dos'. I had a bit of luck when I got an assignment on family life in Northern Ireland. Since then things haven't been going too badly." He paused as the stewardess came by with the drinks cart and ordered two whiskies and sodas. "What do you do? How did you get away?"

"Sheer luck! I teach at a local private school which has just been closed because of measles. The boys have been either sent home or quarantined as the thing really ran wild. I've had measles so I suddenly found myself with the three weeks up to the Easter holidays completely free."

"Rome at this time of the year won't be so thrilling."

"Rome is marvellous at any time. I want to draw and paint and just look for three or four solid weeks." Anne didn't know why, but suddenly she found herself telling Tom the other reason for her visit to Rome. Perhaps it was because he was a journalist and used to extracting information from people in a relatively painless way. She took the letter from her handbag. "Actually, I have other reasons for going to Rome. My sister Laura was married to an American who lives in Rome. His name is Luke Patterson and apparently he's rolling in money. I intend to see him if possible."

"You said 'was'," Tom queried. "Divorced?"

"No. Laura was killed in a car accident three years ago."

"I'm sorry."

"It's all right. We've got over it now. The thing is, six months ago I got this letter from Laura." She waited till his exclamations of surprise were finished and continued. "It was just one of those freaky things that happen sometimes. The letter went to an Andover in the United States and then seemed to wander all over the world before it got to me. Anyway, it eventually reached me almost three years late."

"Must have been weird, getting it like that," Tom observed and Anne nodded vigorously.

"I must say it did give me a bit of a turn."

"What did it say?" he asked, not even attempting to hide his curiosity. "It must have been important to bring you all this way."

"Yes. On the whole it's quite a normal letter, full of news about Luke, her husband, and her baby Lucy, who was just over a year old when Laura died. But the writing is very agitated and the postscript is almost illegible. Listen." Anne opened up the letter and read, "'Oh, Anne, I'm so miserable. I'm absolutely desperate. What can I do? Trying to hide this thing from Luke is driving me crazy. And . . .' there're two lines that I can't read at all. Then she says, 'I've decided to tell him. He'll have to know sooner or later, but he has a terrible temper and after what happened before, I'm sure he'll kill me.'" Anne looked up.

"Dramatic stuff," Tom agreed, and then, softly, "And did he?"

"Did he what?"

"Did he kill her?"

Anne's eyes widened in distress. "Of course not! Really, Tom!"

He shrugged. "I don't know. You said your sister was killed in a car accident, just after writing that, presumably."

"It was dated September 17th and she died in early October. Nevertheless, you're letting your journalistic imagination run away with you."

"Maybe so. But if you don't believe there was anything wrong, why does the letter interest you?"

"I want to know why Laura was so unhappy. She wasn't the sort to get upset in that way, not about anything small. It must have been something serious to worry her so. And I also want to see Lucy, her daughter. She's over four now and I've never seen her."

For a while Tom was silent, staring thoughtfully round the aircraft as though searching for inspiration. Finally he said, "How did the accident happen? It doesn't distress you, does it, to talk about it?"

"No. It was on Capri. I gather Luke has some friends who have a villa there. They were driving down from Anacapri, which is a village about a thousand feet above sea level. The road is narrow and built against a sheer cliff. It's absolutely terrifying. I went there once on a day trip from Sorrento and I closed my eyes most of the way. There are hairpin bends and hardly any kind of crash barrier. In some places the road is actually built out of the cliff on a sort of shelf."

She halted a moment and Tom urged her, "Go on."

"They were driving down this road. It was raining

11

apparently. The brakes failed and the car went over the edge. Luke and Laura both jumped free but Laura fell awkwardly and broke her neck."

"The brakes failed, eh? But you say this road is on the edge of a sheer cliff. There wouldn't be much left of the car."

"No. It burst into flames and exploded."

"So there was just his word for it, that the brakes had gone."

"Yes, I suppose so. But. . . ."

"Was he driving?"

"Yes."

"Hmmm. Sounds interesting."

Somewhat alarmed at what she seemed to have started, Anne rested a hand on Tom's arm. "Look, you can't go round making insinuations of that sort. It's slanderous. Luke is a very important man in Rome. His father owns Patterson and Company, the building firm that has branches all over the world, and Luke is in sole charge of the Continental side. I don't think he would take too kindly to having you put it about that he . . . ," her voice trembled slightly, "that he killed Laura."

She was obviously upset so Tom apologized and tried to drop the subject, but it itched round and round in his brain and he could not leave it completely. A little while later he asked, "What's he like, this Luke bloke?"

"I don't know. I never met him."

"Really? How come?"

"Laura and he met in Italy and they married very

quickly. She never came home again. She ...
wouldn't come home."

"But at her funeral, surely you. ..."

"We didn't go to the funeral. He had Laura
cremated in Rome. I wanted to go but my mother
became ill and I couldn't leave her."

"So you don't know anything about him at all—
what he looks like, how old he is, nothing at all?"

"That's right. Oh, leave it, Tom, please."

For the last half hour of the flight, Anne closed her
eyes and tried to forget about Laura and Luke, and
Tom's probing questions. Yet those questions had
aroused memories. Laura's departure in haste to
Italy and the lights that action shed upon her
selfish, shallow character. Laura the beloved ...
until then. Beautiful, clever, she had sailed easily
through college, emerging with a first-class honors
degree in languages, yet had gone into modeling
because, she said, she couldn't be bothered using
her brain to make a pittance when she could use her
body to make a fortune. Anne was still at school
then, doing her "A" levels. She had loved school;
school was routine and routine was safe. Home was
good too, in those days. Their father was a successful stockbroker working in the city, commuting to
London from his home in Wimbledon each day.
Then, in one short week, one never-to-be-forgotten
July, everything that Anne had known had crashed
around her. The police had come one day, two
serious-faced plainclothesmen, with a search war-
rant. They failed to find Anne's father; somehow he

got wind of the fact that his misdoings had been discovered. That same day he left his office, went to a small hotel in a sleezy part of London where he booked himself a room and there, alone and desperate, he hanged himself. At the inquest it was revealed that he had embezzled over one hundred and fifty thousand pounds over a ten-year period. His wife had a nervous breakdown and tried to kill herself—and Laura had fled to Italy.

It was then that Anne discovered the strength of her paternal grandparents. Heartbroken as they must have been by their son's tragic death, they welcomed Anne into their small home in Andover, cushioned her against more horrors, almost forced her to carry on with her exams, and generally looked after and loved her. When her mother came out of the hospital, a sadly changed woman, they reversed the usual roles and took care of her too. After a relapse caused by Laura's death, she was better now but still inclined to fits of depression and hysteria.

"We're nearly there," Tom said, giving Anne a poke in the ribs. He stared at her. "You're crying."

She touched her face, bringing her fingers away wet. Hastily she wiped her damp cheeks and smiled at Tom's discomfort. "Too many ghosts," she explained. "It won't happen again."

"I should hope not," he muttered gruffly.

"Listen," he said later, when they were in Rome and had gone through the usual routine of passports and customs. "Where are you staying?"

"I don't know. I thought I would wait till I got here. Somewhere not too expensive."

"I'm staying at the Hotel Tiber. It's on the Via Flaminia. Good food, clean, and quite reasonably priced. I usually stay there when I'm in Rome. How about we share a cab?"

Anne smiled. Tom was a good companion and she had a feeling she might need a confidant in the next few days. "Why not?" she agreed.

Rome had decided to prove what it could really do with itself in spring. They sky was a clear blue, softer than the intense blue of summe, with white puffs of cumulus clouds skudding across it, and a gentle, mild breeze ruffled Anne's hair. In the sunshine, Tom now saw, it was not red but gold, the rich, tawny red of Spanish gold. They found a cab which drove them along roads that Tom knew well but which were, to Anne, only names—lovely, Roman sounding names—on a street map: the Appia Nuova, the Via de Pretis, the Via Fontane, Via Sistina, and then, surprisingly swiftly, they were travelling through the Piazza del Popolo and into the Via Flaminia. Anne, her nose pressed against the cab window, exclaimed at her first genuine Roman "sight", an Egyptian obelisk that stood in the center of the piazza.

The Via Flaminia was a street of high apartment buildings, shops, cinemas and the occasional not very fashionable hotel, and the Hotel Tiber didn't look like an hotel. It was narrow and tall, rather dull-looking, and built immediately over an optician's shop. They went into a narrow entrance where there was an elevator up to the reception desk on the first floor. Despite the rather depressing exterior of the hotel, the foyer and bar-lounge were pleasantly decorated and the sun glanced through french windows that led into a courtyard. Tom explained in halting Italian to the receptionist that he wished for two single rooms for at least a fortnight, but he was not called upon to exert himself, for the young Italian clerk behind the desk spoke excellent English. Anne booked her room for two weeks and a further two provisionally.

"It's five-thirty," Tom said as they went up in the elevator. "I'll meet you for a drink before dinner in about an hour. Okay?"

Anne nodded. Her room was pleasantly, if not luxuriously, furnished. Perhaps homely was the best word for it. But the furniture was adequate and there was a small bathroom and a balcony overlooking the Via Flaminia. She stood out on this for a few minutes, straining to look down the road in the direction of the Piazza del Popolo, before pulling out her road map and discovering exactly where she was. Apparently the Via Flaminia was merely an extension of the Via del Corso, which was useful because it was just off this famous thoroughfare that Luke Patterson lived. Perhaps, she thought, soaking off the dust of the journey in a hot bath, she could wander down there after dinner and find out where the apartment was. Then she could call on

the 'morrow when she was rested and more prepared. Thoughtfully, pulling on her dressing gown,
having towelled herself vigorously dry, she took
from her bag Laura's letter and re-read it, trying as
she had hundreds of times, to decipher the two lines
that seemed so important, but failing as usual.
Then she took out of her wallet purse the photo of
Lucy. It was a colored studio portrait of the child
taken when she was about eighteen months old,
sent by her father after Anne's mother had requested one. This was before she began to demand
that he should send Lucy herself. The photo showed
a lovely child with thick blond hair and dark eyes;
she was smiling happily at someone to the left of
her. Lucy was not, Anne thought, much like Laura,
who had had green eyes and reddish hair like her
own. She wondered if Lucy took after her father.

Two

Because the evening, though fine, was likely to be chilly, Anne dressed herself in a two-piece suit she had bought just before coming away. It consisted of a dark green pleated skirt and jacket to match, and was very becoming on her. She put on comfortable brown slingback shoes and went down to meet Tom. He was already at the bar drinking campari soda, and smiled appreciatively at her appearance.

"What will you drink? Same as me?"

"No thanks. Campari is too bitter for me. I'll have a dry martini and soda, please." Anne seated herself on the bar stool beside Tom. "It's a nice friendly sort of hotel. I'm glad we came here."

"Me too. I mean, I'm glad you decided to come with me." He laughed and Anne told him that she intended looking for the Patterson apartment that evening. She got out her map again and showed him where it was situated.

"The apartment is there," she said, pointing. "If I go and take a look, I can look at the Piazza del Popolo on the way."

"You oughtn't to wander round Rome by yourself at night," Tom said quickly. "I'll come with you."

"All right. Thanks. If you're sure you want to."

"Positive. Look," he said, pointing to the map. "If we go down there and cut through the Via dei Condotti we can look at the Spanish Steps. Then along here and into the Via Veneto. Fancy a drink at the Café de Paris?"

Anne laughed. "Idiot! We can't possibly afford it."

"We can afford one small drink each. See how the other half lives. People come to Rome in the winter, you know, when there's not much doing on the Riviera. We might get a glimpse of a film star or two. How about it?"

"Why not?" Anne said gaily, her eyes shining. "I said when I left home that this would be the adventure of a lifetime. Completely free to do as I like in Rome. Why the heck shouldn't we have a drink in the Café de Paris if we want one?"

After dinner, a plain but good meal that satisfied them both, they followed the route laid out for them by Tom. Although the Piazza del Popolo was floodlit, they did not linger there long but set off down the Via del Corso which was well-lighted and they soon found the apartment building where Luke Patterson lived. It was tall and imposing as were all the surrounding buildings, rather palatial with balconied windows that were shuttered.

"Laura lived on the second floor." Anne said, stopping to look up. "I wonder if Lucy is there."

"If she is she'll be asleep now," Tom said practically, taking her arm. "Come on. It's not warm enough to hang about."

At the last minute, in what they both considered to be an extremely cowardly fashion, they funked the Café de Paris but went instead to a scarcely less fashionable, and certainly no less expensive café nearby. Here Tom ordered two martinis and tried not to faint at the price.

"We'll go dutch," Anne said firmly. "No, don't argue, Tom. We're neither of us made of money." Their table was near the window and now she looked out into the well-lighted street. "Here's someone who probably is. Wow! Look at that car. It's half a block long."

Tom looked. "A Cadillac," he said in disgust. "Some people have more money than is good for them." Suddenly he clutched Anne's arm. "Here's our first movie star. Isn't that Elise Carr?"

Anne didn't know Elise Carr though she had heard the name. She looked in frank admiration at the woman who was getting out of the huge gleaming car through a door held open by a uniformed chauffeur. Wearing a long gown of blood-red velvet that clung to a lovely figure, and a little tailored jacket of rich sable across her bare shoulders, she was elegant and graceful. As she moved she sparkled with jewels on wrists, fingers and neck.

"Some blokes have all the luck," Tom muttered.

"Thanks," Anne said with faint sarcasm that was lost on Tom. "She is beautiful, isn't she?" She watched Elise's escort coming round to her from the other side of the car and saw the movie star take his arm. He was tall and fair haired and wore a dinner jacket. Anne said, more or less to get back at Tom, "He looks a bit of all right, too."

"Both out of our class, love," Tom sighed, pulling a face at her. He raised his glass mockingly. "To 'the other half'."

"To the other half," Anne agreed. She raised her glass, clinking it against his, and looked past Tom just as Elise Carr and her escort came into the café. Briefly, as sometimes happens between perfect strangers, Anne's eyes met his. It was not her own reaction, one of acute embarrassment, that puzzled Anne, so much as his. He stared at her in what surely was sheer astonishment, his eyes widened and she was positive his face paled beneath the deep sun tan. This happened very quickly and next moment he and Elise had swept on down the long room. But Anne knew she had not mistaken that look. She met Tom's eyes with puzzlement to match his own.

"What was all that about?" he demanded.

"*Goodness knows.*"

"Do you know him?"

"Of course not. How could I know someone like that?"

"I don't know, but he certainly seemed to know you. He looked like he'd seen a ghost. Sure you don't know him?"

"Positive." Anne finished her drink quickly.

"Come on, let's go," she said. She discovered she was more shaken than she cared to admit by that strange, inexplicable incident. Her one desire was to get out in the fresh air.

"We could have another drink," Tom suggested.

"No!" He quirked one eyebrow at her vehemence and she managed a smile. "It's silly to spend so much money. We've made our point. Let's finish off back at the hotel. It's quite a long walk back and we can have about three drinks there for the price of one here."

The logic of this struck Tom forcibly. "Okay," he agreed, finishing off his own drink. As she stood up, Anne could not resist a quick look towards the table where Elise Carr sat with her escort. Their heads were close together as he lit her cigarette and neither of them looked up. Anne met Tom's glance and shrugged. "He must have mistaken me for someone else," she said quietly.

Anne was up early the following morning, finding herself the first of the hotel's scattering of guests to be down for breakfast. It was pleasant to breakfast alone; she enjoyed the fresh crusty rolls and peach jam, the hot delicious coffee made as only the Italians can make it. As she ate she wondered when the best time would be to call at the Patterson household and finally decided that ten-thirty would be a reasonable time to find most people about. It was a Saturday, which perhaps meant that Luke Patterson would be in. She would, she decided, say merely that she was holidaying in Rome, that she thought she ought to look up her brother-in-law and niece. Patterson's letters to her mother had been none too friendly so she wasn't sure what her reception would be, but surely he couldn't blame her for her mother's hysterical correspondence.

She had finished breakfast when Tom came down, and one look at his appearance convinced her that he was not a good riser. She had always been quite happy to get up early and never felt any different, even at seven in the morning, from at any other time of the day, but Tom looked gloomy and disgruntled, not nearly as garrulous as he had been the previous day. Wisely Anne left him alone and went to her room to write some postcards she had bought at the reception desk.

When the cards were written and stamped, Anne stood before the full length mirror, critically examining her appearance. She was nervous of the approaching interview and reasoned that her confidence would be increased if she felt she looked her best. To this end she had put on one of her new dresses, for it was another warm, blue-skied day and a light summer dress was definitely in order. The dress was denim blue with a fitted bodice that showed off her narrow waist, a semiflared skirt and short sleeves. She brushed her hair till it shone and applied just the faintest of make-up, slipped on a pair of wedge heeled sandals and decided that there was nothing else she could do to improve the look of herself.

It was only just after nine, time for a quiet stroll

before going to the apartment on the Via del Corso. Having seen Tom and told him she would meet him in the hotel at lunchtime, she set out towards the Piazza del Popolo. Her brief visit to Rome some years earlier had not brought her this far north, so now she took out her guidebook and did the tourist "bit" thoroughly. It was an impressive piazza, she thought, as she took her life into her hands and walked across the wide streets while the mad Roman drivers screeched past her. On two sides, high up, were arches and statues and cool, refreshing fountains, and in the center, where six roads met, stood the obelisk which, said her guidebook, came from the time of Rameses II in the 13th century B.C. Anne made a face at this astonishing fact, for the obelisk was in a remarkably good condition, at the same time refusing to catch the eye of the Caribinieri officer who was eyeing her with admiring interest from the door of a Caribinieri station at one corner of the piazza.

It was now ten o'clock and Anne was beginning to feel slightly sick, a sensation generally associated with exams and job interviews. There was a bar just off the piazza with tables and chairs outside on the pavement, the proprietor evidently hoping that summer had come to stay. Anne sank down on a chair, ordered a capuccino and assiduously read her guidebook. The capuccino with its sprinkling of ground dark chocolate was delicious and the drinking of it took her up to ten-twenty, when she thought she might reasonably walk down the imposing Via del Corso which began nearby between two attractive identical churches, to the apartment of Luke Patterson.

The door was opened by a trim, dark-haired Italian maid wearing a black dress and frilly white apron. The sight of the old fashioned uniform took Anne by surprise so that she forgot her carefully prepared speech in Italian and merely blurted out, "Is Mr. Patterson in?"

The maid seemed to understand the English words but her reply, "Si, signorina. Come si chiama?" was beyond Anne. She looked blank.

"Your name," explained the girl.

"Oh . . . name," Anne said and then the maid laughed. "Si. Your name, please."

"Miss Anne Markham," Anne said and the maid repeated this before disappearing, but leaving the door slightly ajar. Through the half-open door, Anne glimpsed a long elegant hall carpeted in rich gold. The walls were painted white with a border of decorated stucco edged with gold. Curious, Anne gave the door a little push; now she glimpsed an Italian marble-topped hall table that supported a tall, slender vase of Chinese design, and a full length mirror that threw her own reflection back at her. There were several doors leading off the long hallway, each painted white and with the same delicate gold embellishment. Anne heaved a little sigh. Her short language tussle with the maid had temporarily robbed her of her fears, but in the face of this obvious wealth and luxury they came flooding back.

Anne Neville

From behind one of these many doors, a masculine voice said loudly, "Good God!" A moment later the maid appeared, saying, "Please will you come in, signorina?" and Anne stepped inside, treading delicately upon the thick piled golden carpet just as Luke Patterson came out of a room some way down the hall.

It seemed to Anne later, when she was able to think more clearly, that somehow, in some indescribable way, every moment in her life had led up to this point. It was as though she was suspended in time, floating in a cloud that was a mixture of curiosity, fear and attraction. This, she accepted, was all in retrospect. At the time she was aware only of two things; first that this was the same man who had stared at her in the café on the Via Veneto the previous evening, and secondly that he was even now staring at her in much the same way—with frank astonishment.

He said, still standing about ten yards away from her, "Are you Laura's sister?"

"Yes," she replied softly. "Are you . . . Luke?"

"I am." There was a brief pause then he said, "I suppose I should be glad you *weren't* a ghost. What do you want?"

The question, and the ungraciousness of it, threw Anne completely. She discovered she was floundering badly. "I was . . . I mean, I'm on holiday in Rome and I thought that I. . . ."

"In March?" he demanded incredulously.

"Yes. It's quieter . . . and cheaper!" This brittle,

26

defensive statement seemed to be what was needed; surprisingly, despite his obvious wealth, he understood her logic. He also noticed how in seconds he had reduced her from a tall, elegant young woman to a tongue-tied schoolgirl.

"You'd better come in," he said more reasonably, and she walked towards him and through the door that he held open.

The room was beautiful. The carpet was silver-grey and the curtains at the long rectangular windows a deep royal-blue velvet hanging to the floor. Every piece of furniture appeared to have been carefully chosen to combine in delightful harmony though of many different styles and periods, from the Queen Anne chairs to the lovely rosewood card table that stood by one wall, and the mahogany bureau that was open and at which Luke Patterson had obviously been working. Anne was entranced. She knew very little about antique furniture but her artistic training had given her an unerring eye for that which was good and tasteful, and she instinctively knew that everything in the room had been collected by a connoisseur, yet someone who believed that beautiful things were to be used and lived with, not locked away in a museum.

"What a lovely room!" she cried out, forgetting to be nervous, and had the satisfaction of seeing a faint smile take away the sternness from Luke Patterson's mouth. He indicated a chair and Anne sat down, slowly regaining her poise. He stood before her, studying her face in a detached way, and after a moment she risked looking up at him. She had been prepared for a lot of things—for bad temper, for aggression, anger, arrogance; she had not been prepared for the sheer blinding good looks of the man. Attractive men frightened her—always had done. She was much happier and at ease with nice, ordinary men like Tom Edwards. And now inside her she shrank away from Luke Patterson. Her sudden appearance here had presumably put him out a little, but she had no doubt that if he wanted to he could switch on the charm. She was thoroughly dismayed. He wasn't a *bit* like she had expected. He didn't look like a successful business-man. She didn't know what he looked like. Yet perhaps she oughtn't to feel so surprised. She should have expected the man that Laura married to be something out of the ordinary. He was abso-lutely Laura's type of man, tall and handsome in a distinguished way, and brimming over with self-confidence that only money and good looks can produce.

"Will you have a drink?" he asked politely, indi-cating a drinks cart.

"No, thank you."

"It is a little early, I guess. Coffee then?"

"Thank you," she murmured and watched as he picked up a telephone and spoke into it in rapid, fluent Italian. She watched him covertly. Laura had always given the impression, in the few letters she wrote home, that he was an older man, but he couldn't be much older than Laura would have been, had she lived. That is, thirty-four. He moved like a young man; dressed in grey trousers and a red and white check shirt open at the neck he was virile and strong-looking. She noticed the width of his shoulders and the muscular appearance of his arms where they protruded from the rolled up shirt sleeves.

He took up an attractive cigarette box from the bureau and handed it to her before taking one himself and lighting both with a gold and onyx table lighter. "I don't quite understand," he said in a deep, slow voice that held just a trace of an American accent. "Laura mentioned you, of course. Anne, isn't it? And I gathered you were a little younger than she was, but not all that much younger."

Anne blinked her green eyes at him, puzzled. "Laura was ten years older than me."

He worked that one out swiftly and his eyes widened. Then slowly he smiled. As smiles went it was pretty devastating and Anne gulped and drew hard on her cigarette. "Do you mean to tell me you're twenty-four?" he demanded incredulously.

"Yes. Why?"

"I wasn't even sure whether to offer you a cigarette. You look about sixteen."

"I can assure you I'm not!" Anne cried indignantly and he laughed. At least this misconception had broken the ice and Anne found herself beginning to relax. He had never been anything but relaxed after the first astonished reaction on seeing her. The maid brought in coffee, served in a lovely bone china

29

coffee pot with matching cups that looked too fragile to use, and he asked Anne to pour.

"Black for me. No sugar." Luke looked down at the bent head; her red-gold hair fell softly in two sweeping curtains either side of her face as she leaned forward to pour out the coffee. Curious how . . . vulnerable the back of a woman's neck could be. A little line of soft blond hairs ran down her spine . . . abruptly he sat opposite her and said, briskly, "Where are you staying?"

"The Hotel Tiber."

"And where," he inquired, "is the Hotel Tiber? I've never heard of it."

"Oh, *you* wouldn't," Anne said without rancor. "It's on the Via Flaminia. It's not much to look at and it's cheap and fairly good—so far anyway."

"You keep on about cheapness. What the heck were you doing on the Via Veneto if you don't have much money?"

"We were just . . . ." Anne hesitated and then grinned at the thought, remembering Tom's words. "We were just seeing how the other half lives." Their eyes met and they smiled at each other. His eyes were brown, not the blue that should go with that thick mop of straw-colored hair, and fringed with long dark lashes. How odd, Anne thought, that last night he was one of the "other half," one of the sort that Tom had said was out of their class. Yet now, for a moment, no matter how briefly, she and Luke Patterson were on the same side.

"How long have you been in Rome?" he inquired.

"Since yesterday."

"You didn't waste much time coming here." There was dry, faint sarcasm in his voice and Anne flushed.

"I suppose not. I wanted to see . . . where Laura lived." She had changed the end of the sentence and now cursed herself for being a coward and added, "And I'd like to see Lucy, please."

He didn't answer at once but stared at her suddenly strained face in vague puzzlement. Finally he said, "Why the intensity, for God's sake? Sure you can see her."

"Oh! Thank you!" Her smile was so wide and so obviously relieved that his puzzlement increased. Did she think he was likely to refuse to let her see Lucy? He glanced at his watch.

"Come on. I'll take you in now."

Anne followed him out into the hall and across to another door from behind which the shrill tones of a child could be heard. He opened the door and stood back so that Anne could walk past him. In its way the nursery was as delightful as the room from which Anne had just come. It was decorated in the way of so many nurseries with pictures of animals and toys all over the walls, and a quick glance told Anne that materially Lucy had everything a child could wish for. She saw a magnificent rocking horse with fiery nostrils and flowing tail and mane, a Wendy House, sundry dolls, painting easel and various other toys. A second glance told her that Lucy had more than just material comfort. Here was a loved child. She was sitting at a large table drawing, while a young woman sat beside her offering advice. This girl, dressed in a white nylon overall, stood up as they entered, smiling and speaking a greeting in soft Italian. Lucy, meanwhile, uttered a screech of delight, clambered down from her chair and rushed to her father who lifted her high above his head, laughing with her.

There were countless facets to a person's character, Anne thought. It was no wonder there were so many misunderstandings in the world. Already she had seen two very different sides to Luke Patterson—the cold, emotionless man who had first greeted her, the cool, charming, virile man who had caused her heart to do so many strange things . . . and now the loving, gentle man who was Lucy's father. She discovered this was the side of him that seemed to her the most delightful, perhaps because it was also the safest. She smiled as he and his daughter talked, faces close together. Lucy was four years old, a lovely, older edition of the child in the photo Anne had. Her blond hair, the same color as her father's, was tied in two bunches and she wore a straight, short dress of blue gingham.

Impulsively Anne said, "Oh, she's exactly like you!"

Luke's head jerked round and he stared at her; for a brief moment there was something in his dark eyes that she could in no way understand. It wasn't surprise, or pleasure, or anything else that she could interpret. "Is she?" he asked slowly.

"Yes. Can't you tell?"

"No. I guess it's not easy to tell a thing like that yourself."

"I suppose not. But she seems to be more like you than like Laura."

While they talked, Lucy turned to look at Anne, her cheek pressed against Luke's. She smiled shyly at Anne, and Anne wanted suddenly, almost like a pain, to reach out and grasp to her this child, this daughter of Laura's . . . and Luke's.

"Lucy, this is . . . ." Luke hesitated, then grinned. "Your Aunt Anne, I guess, though she doesn't look old enough to be anyone's aunt. She's come to see you."

"Hello Lucy," Anne said softly.

"Hello."

There was a moment's silence, then Lucy wriggled and Luke put her down. They watched as she ran over to her rocking horse and climbed on, beginning to rock back and forth in a wild manner.

"Anne, this is Gianetta, Lucy's . . . well, I don't know what she is—nurse, nanny, teacher. She's been with her since she was born. Gianetta, my wife's sister, Anne."

"Buon giorno, signorina," Gianetta said formally.

Anne murmured one or two commonplace remarks and then Luke said, "We'll leave you to it," and turned away. Anne said, quickly, "Oh, could I . . .?"

"What?"

"Do you mind if I stay a little while?"

"Of course not. Gianetta, let me know when Signorina Markham is leaving."

"Si, signore."

When he had gone the two women eyed each other speculatively then Gianetta relaxed her stiff attitude and smiled broadly. She spoke good English with a pleasant, lilting accent. "It is nice that you come, signorina. I say often to Mario, he is my fiancé, that Lucy must have a family somewhere, Signora Patterson's family. And you, you are like Signora Patterson."

"Am I?" Anne asked in astonishment.

"Oh, yes. It surprises me a moment when you came in, but I was not shocked for Gina told me you are here. Gina is the maid. She is my sister."

"Ah. I thought there was a resemblance."

"My Mario also works for Signor Patterson. He gave me the job because he knows we are saving to be married, and also Gina, who is always short of money. And mia madre—my mother—she is a widow and she is Signor Patterson's housekeeper."

"Quite a family affair," Anne smiled. Lucy had left the rocking horse and was now elbow deep in her sand tray. With one accord Anne and Gianetta knelt to play with her, but still chatting together over the blond head.

Gold In Her Hair

"See, Lucy, this is a good sandcastle, yes? And have you met Signor Patterson before today, signorina? He is a very good man to work for, very generous and friendly, you know? And so handsome!" Gianetta laughed. "When first I bring Gina here to work, she fall head over heels in love with him! She is a dreamer, that one, who spends much time at the movies, and she says Signor Patterson looks like Robert Redford."

"Really?" Anne laughed.

"You know of this Robert Redford? He is an American movie star. Me, I do not go to the movies so I could not say. But Gina, she says Signor Patterson is so beautiful."

Anne grinned. "I don't somehow think he would appreciate that description."

"Men do not like to be called beautiful, though I do not see why. I think my Mario is beautiful. Gina, now, she has these crazy ideas about Signor Patterson. Till I tell her, she has no chance. A man like that would have a great pick of lovely and famous women. And now there is Signorina Carr. You know this lady? She truly *is* a movie star. Elise Carr she is called."

"Yes, I know her," Anne said hollowly. She looked down at Lucy's gleaming hair. Although she could not say why, she had no wish to talk about Luke and Elise Carr. "Come on, Lucy, show me your Wendy House."

She was relieved that Gianetta was agreeable to changing the subject. Thereafter they talked to and about Lucy. Anne, who had never had much to do with young children, preferring the children of twelve to fifteen years that she taught, was astonished at the immediate rapport that sprang up between herself and this newly discovered niece of hers. Gianetta moved into the background, taking the opportunity to tidy up some cupboards, and Anne took Lucy upon her lap and told her "The Tale of the Turnip." Lucy watched her face the whole time, looking up at Ann through Luke's eyes, one hand gently holding a handful of Anne's hair which she occasionally rubbed against her soft pink cheek.

"Say it again," she requested when Anne was finished. "Say about the little old man, the grandfather and the little old woman, the grandmother and the little girl, the. . . ." She hesitated over the word.

"The granddaughter," Anne supplied.

"The granddaughter. Say it again."

"It is midday, time for Lucy's lunch," Gianetta said, coming over to them. She had enjoyed listening to the story herself. "Perhaps, Lucy, if you ask nicely, Signorina Anne will come again."

"Will you?" Lucy inquired, widening her eyes.

"Yes, of course I will." Anne set the child down and stood up, glancing at her watch. "Good heavens, I shall miss lunch if I don't get going. Thanks, Gianetta. I've really enjoyed this morning."

"It is good for Lucy to meet people, signorina. Please come again soon."

"I'll certainly try to." Anne bent down to Lucy and smiled at her. "See you again, young 'un, and we'll have another story. Right?"

"Right," Lucy agreed gravely.

"Bye bye, then, love."

"Bye bye." Anne kissed Lucy's soft cheek and received a kiss in return.

"I will tell Signor Patterson you are leaving," Gianetta said.

Luke met Anne at the door of his study. "Stay to lunch?"

There was nothing Anne would have liked better, but equally she knew too well that it was unwise to have too much of his company in one go. It would be, she decided, not unlike an overdose of radiation.

"Thanks. But I more or less arranged to meet someone back at the hotel."

"The guy you were with last night?" he asked, or rather, it seemed to Anne, demanded. He sounded a little on edge. Probably he wasn't used to being turned down for someone like Tom.

"Yes," she agreed. "Tom Edwards."

"You came to Rome with him?"

"No. We met on the plane." Anne immediately wished she hadn't said that. It sounded as though she had allowed Tom to pick her up. Quickly she added, "We got talking and he knew about the hotel. I hadn't booked anywhere, you see. I've never been abroad alone before and it was nice to know someone."

"Of course," he agreed. He reached out to open the

front door for her, but at that moment the bell was shrilly rung so that they both jumped in surprise and then laughed. As Luke reached for the catch, Anne stepped back out of the way so that Luke stood between her and the newcomer.

Luke said, in an astonished voice, "Good God, Simon, what the hell are you doing here?"

"That's no way to greet your long absent brother," a very American voice drawled. "I hoped I'd be more welcome."

It was true that Luke's voice had not held much welcome or warmth. However, remembering Anne's presence, he said quietly, "You'd better come in."

Simon Patterson walked past Luke and his bright, very dark blue eyes alighted upon Anne with great interest. Anne returned the appraisal with a smile. Simon was younger than Luke, possibly in his late twenties, not so tall and very slim, almost willowy. Anne supposed that some women would consider him more handsome, though to her he was not so strikingly attractive. There were certain similarities between the two men—the color of their hair, their smiles—but Anne soon found that she could talk to Simon without any of the confused sense of delight that Luke's presence instilled upon her.

"Who's this then?" Simon demanded, coming up to her, holding out his hand and giving her a long, cool, charming smile. "It looks as though I came just at the right time."

"Anne Markham, Laura's sister," Luke introduced them dryly. "Anne, my brother, Simon."

"Half-brother," Simon corrected swiftly, taking Anne's hand. It seemed an unnecessary distinction to make, almost as though he wanted the relationship between the two of them to be as minor as possible. "Laura's sister, eh? I don't think I knew that Laura had a sister."

"There's no reason why you should have, is there?" Luke said, his voice edgy. Anne glanced between the two men, aware of some undercurrent of tension that flowed between them, wondering what it could be. There was definite animosity in Luke's eyes and voice, and Simon seemed to find this amusing.

"How long are you here for?" Luke asked. He made no attempt to go any further into the apartment but remained solidly immovable, hands in trouser pockets, by the still-open door. It occurred to Anne that he was probably waiting for her to go.

"A couple of weeks." Simon's eyes met Anne's in appreciation. "Or maybe longer . . . now. How long are you staying in Rome, Anne?"

"I don't know for certain. Three or four weeks I hope."

"Then I'm sure I'll see you again." The smile he gave her was so obviously intended to impress and charm her that it failed to do either. Anne thought he was probably great fun, a wonderful companion to laugh with, but no girl in her right senses would get serious about Simon Patterson. He ought, she thought, to take a few lessons from Luke if he wanted to cause a girl's heart to behave irrationally.

Simon turned away from her to look at his brother. "I'm staying at the Grand," he announced. Luke made no answering comment. Considering the apartment was so large that there obviously were several spare bedrooms, it seemed that Simon was waiting to be invited to stay there, but Luke made no such suggestions and a flicker of annoyance crossed the good-looking face of the younger man. Then he went on, casually and in a friendly tone, "Where's Lucy?"

"Having her lunch in the nursery."

"I'll go in and see her then. I have something for her. I hope to see you again, Anne, very soon." Anne watched the slender figure go off down the hall and then turned to take her leave of Luke. She was totally unprepared for the look of naked fury on his face. He was looking at the departing back of his brother as though he could willingly tear him limb from limb.

"I think I'd better go," she said uncertainly, and to her relief the look faded and Luke smiled at her almost apologetically.

"Yes. Sorry about that. I'll get the car brought round to take you back to your hotel."

"Oh no, there's no need. I wouldn't dream of troubling you."

"No trouble. My chauffeur, Giovanni, will drive

you." He picked up the telephone affixed to the wall and spoke into it. "He won't be a moment."

"Thank you," Anne murmured.

"It's just occurred to me that perhaps you might care to come to dinner tonight. A French couple—a business colleague and his wife—will be coming, and a few others." When Anne hesitated, not at all sure that she could handle a high power dinner party, he added, "Bring along that Tom fellow, if you like. It might help since you won't know anyone else."

"All right. Thank you. I'd love to come."

"Fine. At eight then." The phone rang shrilly. He answered it and replaced the receiver at once. "Your car is waiting, ma'am."

"Thank you. I'll see you tonight then."

"Yes. Ciao, Anne."

She walked across the outer hall to the lift, aware that he had not closed the door and was looking after her. The hallway seemed very long. She pressed the button to call the lift, stepped in and turned round. Luke was standing in the doorway still watching her, before he seemed to nod his head in dismissal and closed the door softly.

Why, he's lonely! Anne thought, and immediately scoffed at herself. Idiot! How could a man like that be lonely? Attractive, rich, charming, he could have all the company he wanted. He certainly doesn't need *my* company, she told herself sternly. Just you stop being so ridiculous, Anne Markham. He asked you to stay to lunch because it was the polite thing to do. No doubt he could get far more attractive company just by the lift of a telephone.

And as though to emphasize this fact, as she crossed the pavement to the sleek, silver-grey Cadillac that waited for her, its rear door held open by a blank faced chauffeur, another car drew up behind it, brakes screeching. A white Ferrari it was that halted only inches from the Cadillac's expensive rear. Elise Carr, dressed in skin tight denims and a skinny sweater, the kind of rather scruffy gear that a woman can only get away with if the jewellery she wore was real, got out. For a moment she stared at Anne, her eyebrows raised, before tossing her black curls, loose today and flowing down her back, and flouncing into the apartment building. Anne crawled into the opulent rear seat of the Cadillac, feeling very small and lost in one corner. The car purred softly to life and seemed to float on the air the short distance to the Hotel Tiber. The journey completed, Anne murmured her thanks to the driver and went quickly into the hotel. Above all, she wanted to be alone with her confused thoughts and impressions. Everything was so complicated, she thought miserably. Why couldn't people be the way they were supposed to be, instead of changing and getting things all in a muddle?

Three

Tom was waiting in the bar for Anne. He bought her a martini and then demanded eagerly, "Well, how about it? What did he say?"

Anne frowned. "What did he say about what?"

"About the letter of course! Honestly, love, you did confront him, didn't you? About your sister's death? About the letter and what she said in it?"

As she listened to him, Anne felt dismayed and chill. To admit that from the first moment she had set eyes on Luke Patterson she had forgotten all about the letter sounded infantile and empty-headed. It was true, but she wasn't going to tell Tom that. She said, "I didn't mention it today. I wanted to see how things went. I met Lucy and she's gorgeous, Tom. Such a happy, pretty little girl."

"No worries there then. That's something, I suppose."

"Tom," Anne went on, "you'll never believe it. You remember that man at the café last night—the one with Elise Carr? Well, that's him, that's Luke. He looked shocked because, well, because I look like

Laura. He said he was relieved he hadn't actually seen a ghost."

"Ah!" Tom said, his tone full of meaning that completely eluded Anne. "Ghosts only haunt the guilty, my girl, and only the guilty are aware of ghosts."

"What in heaven's name does that mean?"

"I mean, if Luke Patterson killed your sister, naturally he'd be frightened and. . . ."

"No!" Anne cried. Her hand, in the process of reaching for her drink, jerked and the full glass went flying. There was a brief skirmish as she and the floor were mopped up and her glass was replenished. Horrified at such thoughts, especially after having met Luke, Anne said, "Tom, you mustn't spread these things about. It's pure speculation, unfounded in fact. Luke talks perfectly normally about Laura. Please, please don't mention it again."

"Of course I won't spread it around. But I'm a journalist, Anne, and I'm curious. You've whetted my appetite. While you've been gallivanting round I've been doing a bit of digging too and I've been finding out about Luke Patterson."

Anne's mouth was dry. "What have you found out?"

"Just a few biographical facts so far. He's the eldest son of Keith Patterson, a millionaire who made his money by inventing some new form of ceiling, all to do with having heating, ventilation and what-not, all in one unit. It's a bit technical but I gather it went down big in the States and Canada and latterly all over South America and Europe. About three years after Luke was born his mother died and old Keith picked up a real young dolly bird who gave him another son, Simon."

"I met Simon today," Anne volunteered reluctantly.

"Is that right? He normally runs the family business in Canada while Luke deals with the whole of Europe. Anyway, the old man is a recluse. No one has seen him for the last five or six years. He's likely to pop off any minute and when he does, well, your Luke is going to be a very rich man. Or Simon, of course. Which ever one happens to be in favor. It seems the old man is very fond of changing his will."

Anne said flatly, "I don't know why the private lives of these people can be of interest to you, Tom. What has it got to do with us anyway?"

"I like to know people, that's all. I also found out that your sister's accident was played way down. It only merited a small paragraph in the papers."

"So what? I don't see that. . . ."

"Oh, come off it, Anne! An accident like that should get much better coverage. But Patterson is a very rich man with or without his father's millions. In a country like this, if you have enough money and prestige, it isn't hard to keep the papers quiet."

"Oh, God, this is terrible. Tom you must stop this!" Anne cried. "I wish I'd kept my big mouth shut."

"What's the matter with you, Anne?" Tom demanded. "Yesterday you were all for finding out the

45

truth. Now you just want to shut out the facts. You haven't fallen for the bloke, have you?"

The color rushed into Anne's face. "Don't be stupid," she muttered in a stifled voice. "I just realize since meeting him that the whole thing is ridiculous, just a product of my over-active imagina-tion. It just isn't possible." She put one hand over his as it lay on the arm of his chair. "Please, Tom, don't go on with this."

He had already set one or two minor wheels in motion, but seeing her obvious distress, he did not enlighten her. Maybe nothing would come of it, but he was a journalist through and through and couldn't resist probing a bit. When, later, she told him about the dinner party that evening he was delighted at the chance of getting a close look at Luke Patterson and forming a judgement of his own. He promised faithfully to be on his best behavior and to make no mention of Laura's death or the letter. By the time they had finished their lunch Anne was smiling again and Tom suggested that for the afternoon they should remember why they were really in Rome, that was, for sightseeing. Anne went up to her room to change into her one and only pair of denim jeans.

"Where to first?" Tom asked.

"Saint Peter's. I want to climb to the top of the dome. All six hundred and something steps, so stop groaning about it. You can stay below if you like."

"I was groaning because I've done it before, only

then the lift was working to take us a fair part of the way. Maybe it will be today."

Anne linked her arm in his. "Then I suggest we get a move on, or there won't be time to see anything. I told Luke we'd be there by eight so we must get back by six to get ready."

The lift was not working, but though Tom complained, he trudged after Anne up the five hundred and thirty-seven steps. The climb was not continuous. Before the dome itself was entered they were able to go out on to the roof of the basilica to view the huge statues of Christ, John the Baptist, and the Apostles, each over sixteen feet high, that crowned the basilica, gazing down upon Saint Peter's Piazza. From here, looking down over the stone balustrade, Anne gazed in wonder across the piazza with its Egyptian obelisk and two fountains and straight down the Via Conciliazione. It was a breath-taking view and Anne was entranced. Immediately before them was the stubby circular shape of the Castel Sant'Angelo, and beyond that, a sweep of the Tiber glinting blue in the sunshine.

"It's better than ever from the top," Tom told her. "And as for the climb, the worst is yet to come. Come on, I hope you don't mind heights."

"Of course I don't," Anne said confidently.

There was now a narrow spiral staircase and then, after another brief pause for breath, some more narrow steps and this time it was obvious that they were actually climbing within the dome itself. The steps went clockwise round the cupola and the walls sloped to the right following the curve of Michaelangelo's magnificent dome. The climbers were themselves forced to lean to the right also and Anne was just beginning to wonder if they would ever reach the top when they did. There before them was a ladder stretching vertically above their heads. There was a short wait as only sixteen people were allowed up there at one time, but soon it was their turn to venture up to a small, circular balcony just below the ball of the cupola. The cold wind hit them as they emerged into the sunlight and Anne gasped.

They were standing literally on top of the dome which fell away beneath their feet and increased the sensation of great height. For a moment Anne hesitated, her back pressed against the central part of the balcony, the only part that seemed safe, not daring to venture near the seemingly fragile railing. Tom turned and looked at her.

"Not scared of heights?" he inquired, grinning, and held out a hand to her. "Come and look."

Anne took a deep breath and obeyed. Now not only Saint Peter's Square but the whole of Rome lay before them. A Rome of pink tiled roofs, gleaming cupolas, tall white hotels, and everywhere masses of greenery. They walked slowly round the full circle of the gallery, looking down upon where they had previously stood, so high above the basilica roof now that even the huge statues seemed tiny, and even further away, coaches, cars and people were like black ants crawling about. On another side they could look down directly upon the gardens of the Vatican palace, green and luxurious.

"That's the Vatican city railway," Tom told Anne, pointing. "We should go round the Vatican museums before we go home. You'll want to see the Sistine Chapel, of course, and the other treasures are well worth looking at. Besides, everyone sends postcards home with the special Vatican stamps." He glanced down at Anne who was clutching the railing with tight, white knuckled fingers.

"Anything wrong?"

"No. It's just . . . it's all so . . ." she laughed shakily. "I'm lost for words. But I'm also scared. I never suffered from vertigo before. But then, I've never before been so high."

"Let's go down then," Tom suggested. "Though I warn you, it's harder going down than it was coming up!"

"Thanks for that small comfort," Anne said dryly.

Once they were down on firm ground again, there was time for a quick tour of the church itself. Although they had both been in there before, there were certain things, Anne decided, that could never be looked at often enough. Her own footsteps led her to the Pietà, the white marble statue by Michaelangelo of the Virgin with the crucified Christ in her arms. Fully restored now after the vandalism perpetrated upon it some years earlier, it looked as perfect as it had been when Anne first saw it.

"It's the most beautiful thing I ever saw in my

whole life," she whispered to Tom. "Look at her face, Tom, and the hands. When I first saw it I was seventeen and I could have cried because of its beauty. And I still could."

"You don't feel it's been ruined because of what that madman did to it with the hammer?"

Anne shook her head. "I should love to touch it. I can't believe that if I did it would really be cold hard marble."

Tom grinned, a little embarrassed by the fervor in Anne's voice. "It must be the artist in you," he said, and then, "We'd better go. It's almost five o'clock."

"Yes, all right. I have plenty of time to come again. Thanks for being so forbearing, Tom."

"I've enjoyed it," he answered. "Even if I did moan."

Tom, very smart in a dark lounge suit, was waiting for Anne at seven-thirty when she came down from her room. He admired her orange and brown floor length dress and the way she had pinned up her hair into a more sophisticated style that made her look older. She had varnished her fingernails orange and wore matching lipstick and rather more eye make-up than usual.

"I should have brought my dinner jacket," Tom grinned.

"You look very smart indeed."

"And you look very nice too," he returned. "We'll have a drink, shall we? Dutch courage."

"Do you need it? I'd have thought in your job you'd be used to meeting all sorts of people."

"True, but not socially. When I'm hiding behind pencil and notebook, firing questions at them, it's like wearing a suit of armor and they're at my mercy."

"I'm sure you'll be fine. One flash from the eyes of Elise Carr will put you on cloud seven."

"Oh, will she be there?" Tom asked, innocently.

"I don't know, but I imagine so. From what Lucy's Italian nurse told me, Luke and Elise are pretty close."

Anne was pleased to discover that she could utter this with complete coolness. That morning, and the strange tumult of emotions Luke Patterson had aroused in her, seemed very far away now. In Tom's company she was back in the real world, the world in which men like Luke Patterson did not look twice at girls like Anne Markham. In the normal way Anne was a realist who refused to get herself into a state over something—or someone—that was definitely beyond her grasp. Laura was able to capture such a man as Luke, but then, Laura had been mature, sophisticated, intelligent and, above all, very lovely. While she, Anne, though not unintelligent and at least reasonably attractive, felt naïve and tongue-tied in Luke's company, and hadn't he said she looked about sixteen?

"From what I gathered this morning, he's quite a one for the ladies," Tom said, watching her face closely for any change of expression. She looked interestedly at him.

"That doesn't surprise me. He's a very attractive man, and anyone that wealthy has a head start," she said easily, and Tom decided he must have been mistaken that morning in thinking that after only a couple of hours she had fallen for Luke Patterson.

He looked at his wrist watch. "Time to go. I ordered a taxi, by the way. No point arriving on foot for a do like this."

Four

The door of the Patterson apartment was opened again by Gina who gave Anne a big warm smile and eyed Tom with interest.

"Buona sera, signorina. Will you please come in," she said, taking Anne's jacket.

Evidently they were not the first arrivals for there was quite a lot of noise in the apartment. Gina led them down the hall and opened one of the many doors. Beside Anne, Tom took a deep breath and murmured appreciatively, "Wow! Did you know you could smell wealth?"

Anne giggled. She was still laughing when they entered the large, elegant lounge and Luke came to greet them. He looked, she thought in a confused state of delight, wonderful in a black dinner jacket with a dark blue velvet bowtie over a white silk shirt. He greeted them both with great charm, shook hands with Tom, saw that they were both supplied with drinks and introduced them to his other guests. These were a middle-aged French couple, Monsieur and Madame Flambert, and an Italian couple and their daughter. Anne felt her brain whirl as she listened to the casual, self-confident manner in which Luke made the introductions. So, this was the "society" Luke Patterson. Yet another facet to his character.

Anne had never been very much at ease making light conversation with strangers and now was no exception. She watched Tom turn to talk to Monsieur Flambert and his petite, smart wife in their own language which he spoke remarkably well. The Italians seemed to have very little English and their daughter, who was younger than Anne, joined in the French conversation. For a moment Anne felt rather lost. It was indeed only for a very brief moment for Luke came over to her, taking her bare arm in cool, casual fingers and leading her out of the french windows on to a balcony at the rear of the building. This overlooked a square courtyard illuminated by spotlights, in which a fountain played. The balcony was filled with wooden tubs overflowing with brilliant green plants and spring flowers, flowers that one did not somehow associate with Rome—daffodils, tulips and crocus.

"Oh, Luke, this is lovely," Anne cried, crossing to the ornate wrought iron balustrade. "Who would ever think such lovely things could be hidden away inside these buildings?"

"Not hidden away," he said, joining her. "I don't believe that beautiful things should be hidden away." He was looking closely at her as he spoke, contriving to make the words strangely intimate, as though they had a different meaning entirely from the surface one. Now he smiled at her and said. "I do believe, Anne, you're growing up. Tonight you look at least eighteen." When she made no reply to this comment, other than wrinkling her nose, he added, "Don't you realize there are some women who would give their eye teeth to look eighteen?"

"Not when they're only twenty-four anyway," Anne replied.

"No? What would you like to be then? A sophisticated woman of thirty-five I suppose, draped in mink and dripping with diamonds."

"No. I'm quite happy to be twenty-four, thank you. I wouldn't dare wear real diamonds because I'd be scared of losing them. And as for fur coats, I would never wear real fur. I don't approve of killing beautiful animals just to pamper to rich women's vanity."

He laughed softly though not unkindly. "Oh, Anne, the arrogance of youth! What about the shoes you wear, the handbags you carry? Aren't they made from the skins of animals?"

"That's different—and you know it is! I'm not a vegetarian and by law of nature one creature eats another in order to survive. To wear the skin of an animal killed to eat is sensible. To kill a tiger, a seal, a polar bear for its fur is plain wicked!"

She glared at him, daring him to disagree, and he smiled. "I quite agree with you, so stop looking daggers at me. And when Elise arrives, no doubt draped in fur, please don't lecture her about conservation. It won't do any good."

"I'm hardly likely to, am I? Give me credit for good manners, if nothing else."

"Oh, I give you credit for a good deal more than that," he said softly, and such was the tone of his voice that Anne shivered. He touched her arm with the back of his hand, his touch sending prickles across her skin. "It's a little chilly. Come on inside. I oughtn't to neglect my guests."

"Is your brother coming?" Anne asked as they walked into the saloon which now seemed quite crowded and already thick with cigarette smoke.

Luke's hand hardened momentarily on her arm and then relaxed and he released her. "Simon," he said lightly, "always turns up—like a bad penny."

Anne wasn't sure how to treat this so she decided to take it lightly and laughed. "I liked him."

Luke's dark eyes studied her face a moment, very seriously. "Yes," he said. "I expect you did. But don't like him too much."

It was an odd thing to say. "I don't suppose I will," Anne returned, puzzled.

By eight-thirty the whole party was assembled. Simon Patterson, very splendid if ostentatious in a deep claret corduroy velvet dinner jacket, arrived with Elise Carr whom he seemed to know very well. Elise was breath-taking in a skin tight white gown of heavy silk, her hair piled high on her head, revealing the wonderful bone structure of her face and shoulders. Anne longed to sketch her, in pen and ink perhaps, stark and hard, highlighting every bone and muscle. The arrival of Simon and Elise changed the tone of the party. From a quiet, rather dignified gathering it changed to a lively interchange of gossip. Even the two more elderly couples joined in the laughter that Simon and Elise brought with them.

Simon made straight for Anne and sat beside her on the settee, taking her hand in a gesture of ownership that she found irritating, considering she had only ever exchanged half a dozen words with him. "I'm sure glad to see you here," he added. "And you look real fine. The best-looking girl in the room."

"Nonsense!" Anne said briskly. "Don't talk such rubbish!"

Simon's eyes widened in surprise and then he laughed. "I see. You're not a girl to be flattered, then?"

"I am not!"

"But then, I wasn't flattering, just speaking the truth. Say, have you known Luke long?"

"Only since today."

"Is that right? I wondered where the old devil had been hiding you away. I somehow thought you weren't his type. Luke goes for the sophisticated sort, like Elise there. Now they make a fine couple, don't they?"

"Yes," Anne agreed hollowly. They did too; Elise in that stark white dress, Luke all light and shadow in his black suit and white shirt and the sun bleached blond hair. She felt acutely depressed, which was a mite ridiculous, she told herself sternly, but with very little effect.

At that moment Gina appeared to announce that dinner was ready. It was all very formal suddenly as everyone waited for Luke to lead the way into the dining room. It reminded Anne of the happenings in a Victorian novel and she sat back, rather enjoying the new experience, fully expecting Luke to lead Elise into dinner. Then, by the way things had turned out, she would go in with Simon and Tom with the dark rather colorless daughter of the Italian couple, to whom he had been talking for the last ten minutes.

Instead, Luke came over to her and held out his hand, saying, "Shall we go in, Anne?"

Aware that everyone in the room was watching her, knowing that she had reddened, for she could feel the heat rush over her cheeks, cursing herself for this infantile habit that she thought had been cured but which had been resurrected with Luke's appearance in her life, Anne stood up and put her hand in his. Then he smiled at her and winked so slightly that only she saw, and inside her something eased, as though the elastic that had been tight round her heart had snapped. He tucked her hand into the crook of his arm, his own hand covering hers, and led her through the big double doors that Gina had opened, into the dining room.

It was a room of magnificent proportions; the

long, highly polished mahogany table glistened in soft light from candles that nestled in bowls of waxy white orchids; the flames reflected off silver cutlery and the cut crystal wine glasses. Anne smiled instantly, delightedly. It was like being drawn into a dream, she thought. And then . . . this is like a fairy story, Cinderella perhaps. I am Cinderella and he . . . she glanced up at Luke who was watching her happiness with tender amusement—yes, he was very much a Prince Charming. And I won't even think about twelve o'clock striking, not yet anyway.

Luke led her to her chair; his was at the head of the table and hers on his right. When they were all seated, alternate men and women, Tom was on Anne's right. She wondered if Luke had arranged this so that neither of them should feel too much alone. It was, she guessed, typical of his thoughtfulness. In the event, Tom had eyes only for Elise Carr who sat on Luke's left.

It was only once she was seated that Anne really looked round and saw the portrait of Laura above the marble fireplace. She stared in astonishment at her sister's face, wondering why she was so surprised to see her portrait there. Laura was dressed in a regency style dress of white that shimmered with jewels; her hair was piled on the top of her head and fell in soft ringlets across one bare white shoulder. It was odd that Anne, though remembering with her brain that Laura had been lovely, had forgotten with her emotions. In fact, she now realized, she could hardly remember Laura's face at all. She looked quickly away from the portrait, not wanting to think about Laura at all, and down the table met the dark blue stare of Simon Patterson, who had been watching her every move intently.

Loudly Simon asked the company at large, "Anne is very like Laura, isn't she?" and again Anne felt everyone's eyes upon her and was annoyed with Simon for making this ill considered remark. She saw now that he was laughing at her, obviously amused by her discomfort, but as no one seemed inclined to help her out, said coolly, "No, Simon, I'm not a bit like Laura. Anymore than you are like Luke."

Laughter sprang into Simon's eyes and he raised his wine glass to her. "Salute, Anne."

As the subject of the portrait had been raised, Anne felt able to turn to Luke who had listened in silence to the short interchange between her and Simon, to ask, "Is it a good likeness?"

"Don't you know?"

"Surprisingly, no. I don't remember her. It's eight years since I saw Laura. When was that painted?"

"Just after we were married," Luke said shortly. "More wine, Elise?"

"Thank you, darling." Elise turned her big violet eyes on him with full force that surely ought to have knocked him for six but in fact appeared to have little or no effect. "I don't know why you won't have the thing taken down, Luke. It's surely a little morbid, keeping it there."

He shrugged. "To be honest, Elise, I don't use this

room often and when I do I don't notice the portrait unless someone comments on it. I guess it's just part of the furniture."

"Not very complimentary to her memory, but so sensible. Don't you agree, Miss Markham?" When Anne looked blankly at her, she added, "There's no point a man spending all his life mourning one woman, is there?"

Anne thought the whole conversation rather distasteful and, though Luke did not appear to be bothered, she was sure a change of subject was indicated. With enthusiasm, and forcing Tom to help, she launched into an account of her and Tom's climb to the top of Saint Peter's. Elise immediately looked bored and turned to talk to Signor Patelli who sat on her left, but Luke, after giving Anne a strange little smile that just might have expressed gratitude, joined with her and Tom in discussing the sights of Rome. Thereafter things went more smoothly; the food was as delicious as was the wine; the conversation that went round the table sparkled as much as the wine glasses and the cutlery and the great glistening crystal chandelier that blazed above their heads. Anne supposed she joined in, but afterwards had no notion of what the talk had been about.

After dinner, back in the lounge again and ensconced in a very comfortable armchair, she sipped her coffee and liqueur and thought, "If I'm not careful I shall have drunk too much and then I'll make a fool of myself." Yet she knew that the heady, intoxicated feeling that had brought on this lazy, warm and cosseted sensation had nothing to do with the wine or the brandy. No, here was a far more intoxicating emotion. It was brought on by Luke who had made it perfectly clear that of all the women there, it was she whose company he preferred. Every time she looked round he was close by as though, she thought wonderingly, he wanted her close presence as much as she wanted his. Right now he was sitting on the arm of her chair, his hand resting on its back just behind her head. She was intensely aware that if she moved half an inch her hair would brush against his hand. At this thought she was breathless with a longing she had never before experienced in her whole life; had never before known there could be so delicious a pain. She once before thought herself in love, with a young man who taught in the same school as she, but how hollow and lacking in substance were the sensations he had aroused in her! Luke, with one quick smile, could set her heart behaving in a ridiculous fashion, while poor Alan had aroused nothing by his kisses.

Simon Patterson was watching her interestedly. Anne had been half-aware all evening that he had been keeping a keen eye on her and Luke and now, seeing how he was watching, she attempted to snap herself out of this floating sensation, concentrating hard on the conversation which seemed to be about Tom's work. One of the guests, a big dark American who apparently worked for Luke, was asking Tom whether he was in Rome following up a story.

"No," Tom replied. "This is just a holiday. But of course if anything were to turn up, I'd be after it like a shot."

"Always keep your eye open for any likely story, eh?" the American asked.

"That's about it," Tom agreed. His quick glance flicked across to Anne who was watching him, more alert now, as the gist of his meaning sank in. "I've got one or two ideas, I must admit."

"If it's scandal you're after, I should have said Rome was kind of lacking in that direction this time of the year," Luke said in a deep, lazy voice, and as he spoke Anne felt his hand move very lightly against her hair. She looked up at him and their eyes met and held. . . .

"Do tell us," Simon drawled exaggeratedly. He had seen that quick warning look Anne had thrown at Tom earlier. "What have you discovered? Corruption in high places, maybe, or white slavery, or a murder?"

One or two people laughed at this, but Tom merely shrugged. "Perhaps."

Anne's head jerked, breaking the spell that had, for a moment, had her drifting away again. Sharply she said, "What are you talking about, Tom? You haven't been anywhere since you got here except to the top of Saint Peter's and I hardly think you uncovered any murders there."

During the brief, faintly uncomfortable pause that followed, everyone in the room looked in puzzlement at Anne. She colored up and dropped her eyes, realizing that her vehemence had given a credence to Tom's words that they would not otherwise have had. Finally Elise Carr, who had quite pointedly ignored Anne since the brief interchange about Laura's portrait drawled, "Don't sound so intense, sweetie. Anyone would think he had uncovered a skeleton in your cupboard."

Anne did not reply and after a moment Marie Flambert, sensing her discomfort, came to the rescue with a comment to Luke about the meal they had just had. "You are lucky to have found such a dream of a chef."

"Actually the meal was cooked by my housekeeper, Signora Verdi," Luke replied. He had taken his hand away from Anne's hair and was now sitting with his arms casually folded. Anne felt strangely bereft and was furious with herself for feeling this way about the casual touch of a man she had only met that very morning. The conversation was turned now to the problem of chefs, a problem, Anne thought wryly, that she was never likely to have to face. The other women, however, were soon well-launched and Luke stood up to begin replenishing glasses. He was joined at the cocktail bar by Elise who stood beside him talking softly. As Anne covertly watched, she put one hand on his shoulder and moved close to him, reaching up and whispering something against his ear. He laughed and murmured a soft reply. Anne looked away swiftly, trying to disperse the pain of jealousy by laughing at her own stupidity in falling in love so easily with this man. She hadn't even fought against it; she hadn't even tried to stop herself falling head over heels into something which could only possibly bring her misery and him . . . amusement? No, he was too kind to feel that. More likely he would feel acute embarrassment if he knew. Her eyes, filled with hurt, encountered Tom's. He too had been looking at the couple at the bar, though not with jealousy. More with wondering about Luke Patterson. Was he capable of doing what Laura's letter implied? He wasn't, on the face of it, the sort of guy to fake an accident in order to kill off an unwanted wife. Then again, it was difficult to tell. A once-only murderer, who killed for reasons of passion, was generally just an ordinary person. The thought occurred to Tom that perhaps the thing Laura had been going to tell her husband was that she had been unfaithful to him. How would a man like Patterson react to that. With a slow build-up of anger that finally came to a head on that cliff road on Capri? Or perhaps, Tom thought imaginatively, she had told him while they were actually driving and he had struck out there and then in blind, unreasoning rage.

At this point Tom stopped speculating. And also at this point he caught the look of naked hurt in Anne's eyes. Silly little fool, he thought without rancor, for he was, though attracted to her, in no way in love with her. Fancy falling for a bloke like that! And even more stupid, fancy showing it so obviously. A chap like Luke Patterson could eat two of her for breakfast.

Despite his scorn, Tom felt somehow protective towards Anne. For this reason he now stood up and announced that it was time they went. Anne looked so relieved that he knew he had done the right thing. Everyone demurred, Luke included, but no one seemed all that bothered. They were not, after all, of their world. They did not know the same places or the same people.

Luke said, "I'll call my chauffeur to take you back to your hotel."

"No need," Tom said firmly. "It's not far. I can get a cab."

"That's a little ridiculous since my car is available."

"I'd like a walk," Anne said quickly. "I think I ought to walk off all that lovely wine and brandy." She raised her eyes to Luke's and for a moment again they looked at each other and everyone else, Tom included, faded away. The moment was gone in an instant. Wondering whether she had imagined it, Anne was saying, "Thank you for a lovely evening, Luke," and Tom was endorsing this sentiment heartily. The two men shook hands and suddenly Anne and Tom were outside.

Their eyes met in a long, direct stare then Anne turned abruptly towards the lift.

"You're a bloody fool," Tom said bluntly as they

began to walk up the Corso towards the Piazza del Popolo.

"What do you mean?"

"You've fallen for him."

"I haven't!" Anne cried. "Don't be stupid! How could I? I hardly know the man."

"What's that got to do with anything? It's all a matter of chemistry, all affairs are in the early stages. It's all physical, you know. You probably feel you'd like him to drag you off to bed or something. . . ."

"I don't!" Anne cried, turning to glare at him. "Really, Tom Edwards, if you think I . . . ."

"Oh, all right! Perhaps you haven't actually put it into thoughts, but I bet it's inside your head somewhere. It's all physical, girl. He's a very good looking bloke, I admit that, and filthy rich as well. You'd be queer not to fancy him. But put it in perspective, Anne, for heaven's sake. Don't go falling in love with him."

Anne walked on, her feet tapping hard on the pavement, her head down. She was furious and upset at the same time. "I think you're stupid, Tom. You don't know anything. You think you're a man of the world. What right have you to talk this way to me when all you did all evening was drool over Elise Carr?"

"Sure I did. But I don't mind admitting my interest. I really would like to drag her off to bed."

"Ohhhh!" Anne hissed at him. "You're impossible!"

"Just normal, love. You know your trouble, Anne. You're just like thousands of other girls of your age and upbringing. The permissive age seems to have passed you by. You're narrow-minded and prudish."

"I am not!"

"Yes you are." By this time they had reached the hotel. The argument ceased as they fetched their keys from the reception desk but started up again in the lift when Tom pressed the seventh button and took them straight up to the floor where both their bedrooms were. Anne turned away from him. "I am not," she muttered. "Just because I don't go jumping into bed with absolutely everyone . . . ."

"I bet you don't jump into bed with anyone at all—and you never will unless you can talk yourself into thinking you're in love with them. That's how it is with Luke Patterson, isn't it? You fancy him, but you can't admit it's just sex so you have to wrap it up in love. For God's sake, you can't love someone you've only just met, but you can fancy going to bed with them."

Anne marched out of the lift. At her bedroom door she turned to face him. "You know your trouble, don't you?" she said in an angry whisper. "You're just plain sick. You give everyone your own low morals. I hate you and I hate your rotten theories!"

Tom grinned. "I've really got to you at last, haven't I? You're beginning to grow up, little orphan Annie."

Anne hit him and he kissed her. Despite the skinny look of him he was surprisingly strong and he had both her arms pinned to her sides so that she was unable to move. He kissed her close-mouthed, not with passion or even particular liking, but more as an experiment and when he released her he laughed. "Go to your virginal bed, Anne darling. I'm not really such a bastard, you know."

Five

Anne was wakened by someone knocking on her bedroom door. She struggled up out of a sleep that had been heavy and far from refreshing and peered at her travel alarm clock on the bedside table. It was almost nine o'clock. She scrambled out of bed, pulling on her dressing gown as she crossed the room. When she opened the door it was to see Tom standing there. His foot was in the door before she had time to slam it in his face.

"Journalistic reflexes," he explained cheerfully. "I'm quite used to getting my foot in people's doors."

"Go away. I don't want to talk to you."

"Yes you do. Come on, Anne, I'm sorry. Maybe I was a bit rough on you last night. All that booze and high living went to my head. Look, you've got twenty minutes till breakfast finishes. Come down and have some."

"Since seeing you I've lost my appetite."

"I apologized."

"I heard you. A person doesn't have to accept an apology you know."

Tom sighed and looked martyred. "Haven't you heard the old saying, 'To err is human, to forgive is divine'?"

"Yes, I have. Right now I don't feel very divine."

"I admit I was wrong. Completely wrong, about everything. Will that do? Oh, come on, Anne. I hate bad feeling."

"Then you shouldn't have started it."

"I was worried about you."

"Oh! That's a good one."

"I was, honestly. I just thought you were getting in out of your depth." He smiled disarmingly. "How about breakfast?"

"Oh, go away!" she snapped. "I'll see you downstairs."

"Atta girl!"

Anne pulled on jeans and sweater; all at once she couldn't care less what she looked like. She certainly wasn't going to dress up for Tom. Yet he, in the process of finishing off his breakfast with a cup of coffee, was wearing a suit. Anne sat opposite him and glanced curiously at his clothes. She ordered a pot of tea and asked him, "Where do you think you're going, dressed like that?"

"Not going—been," he said calmly. "It's Sunday. I've been to Mass."

Anne choked. "Mass! You! Don't make me laugh."

He threw her an injured look. "I'll have you know I go to Mass most Sundays. It's the aim of every good Catholic to go to Mass in Saint Peter's."

"I suppose it is." Anne was unsure whether or not

to take him seriously. Certainly this disclosure had robbed her of the remnants of her anger at him. She said uncertainly, "Are you a Catholic then?"

"Yes."

"And have you really been to Mass?"

"Of course." He looked straight at her. "I asked you to forgive me for all that stuff I said last night. Do you?"

"I suppose so."

"Good girl. What do you intend doing today?"

"I'm going to do some sketching. I've ordered a packed lunch. What about you?"

"Didn't I tell you? Simon Patterson asked me if I fancied a game of golf. He's arranging for me to borrow a set of clubs and he's taking me out to his golf club. It's just south of the city somewhere out towards Ciampino airport. He's picking me up at nine-thirty."

"I didn't know you two had got that pally."

"He seemed quite a decent bloke. Anyway, I fancied I might learn something more from him about the set-up there. Did you get the same impression as me that all wasn't well in the Patterson family nest?"

"What do you mean?"

Tom shrugged. "I don't know exactly. Just an impression. I rather fancied that despite the brotherly love act, there isn't really much love lost between Simon and Luke."

Anne had thought this herself but she wasn't going to admit it to Tom. "Brothers don't always get on," she said. "And they aren't terribly alike in character. I shouldn't think there's any more to it than that."

"No, probably not. Still, it could be an interesting morning." He finished his coffee and stood up. "I'll be off. See you this evening. Have a good day."

Anne went to her room and packed her sketchbook and pencils into her big canvas bag along with the packed lunch of rolls, cheese, hard boiled egg and apple that the hotel kitchen had provided. She would stop somewhere at midday where she could buy a drink off one of the many street vendors that abounded in the center of Rome. While she was packing her bag, the loud roar of a powerful car engine took her quickly onto her balcony. She peered down into the street in time to see Tom getting into a brilliant yellow sportscar being driven by Simon. Simon, she reflected, might be the younger son but if he could drive a car like that and stay for two or three weeks at the Grand, he wasn't exactly short of money. The sportscar drove off with another roar and Anne went indoors to finish getting herself prepared for the day.

She tied her hair up in a pony tail and pulled on a denim jacket over her blouse; when she caught sight of herself in the mirror she saw a very different girl from the starry eyed creature who had walked into the dining room on Luke's arm the previous evening. This girl was practical, casual, comfortable. This girl was not going to think about Luke Patterson and the strange enigma that was his complicated, variable personality. Suddenly she grinned, and the grin turned to a chuckle. She saw herself as Luke would see her. Even at her most sophisticated he thought she looked only eighteen. In this gear she would look like a cheeky urchin. Luke wouldn't look twice at her dressed like this.

For a while she could forget about Luke. Who could worry about someone, even someone so maddeningly attractive as he was, when there were such ancient and wonderful marvels to behold? Anne had never before been alone in Rome. Armed with her guidebook, she started off walking down the Via de Babuino to the Spanish Steps where she was persuaded by a long haired American student to buy a welded metal pendant, one of many he had displayed on a velvet cloth at the top of the steps. The pendant was shaped in the zodiac sign of Gemini which was Anne's own birthsign. She sat upon the edge of the fountain at the foot of the steps and drew them flanked by the high palatial buildings and at the top yet another Egyptian obelisk and the Church of the Trinità dei Monti with its well known façade of twin bell towers. By then the sun had pushed its way through a cloud covered sky and was warm on her back. She lit a cigarette and sat for a while as the water sparkled from Bernini's fountain, and watched the people walking to and from church. She realized she was happy. Freedom was a heady thing. She began to walk again, finding her way to the Trevi fountain and tossing a brand new tenpenny piece over her shoulder into the water, thereby assuring herself that she would return to Rome. She made numerous sketches, of Neptune standing aloft in his great sea chariot, and of his sundry attendant figures. The god of the sea began to come to life beneath skillful, rather grubby fingers. Part of her said, slow down, there's a fortnight and more ahead. But then the artist in her was impatient to see, to experience, to feel. She found her way back to the Corso and caught a bus to the Colisseum, but then had to retrace her steps because the bus took her on past the great marble edifice which was the monument to King Victor Emmanuel II, and also past the Forum. The Roman Forum was her final defeat; there was too much to see, too much that cried out to be included in her sketchbook. She had a surfeit of pillars, arches, columns and temples. Exhausted, she sat down upon the ancient ruins and ate her packed lunch. Having washed down the meal with a can of orange squash she had bought earlier, she leaned back against a pillar and gave herself up the enjoyment of being here, surrounded by history that her imagination brought to life.

In a little while Anne opened her sketchbook once more and began idly to make numerous little sketches, imaginatively now, the place where she now sat as it might have been, complete and new, peopled by tiny figures in togas and tunics. The figures pleased her and she smiled to herself as she turned the page and began again to draw, her fingers gentle now, using a soft pencil, occasionally smudging a line that was too hard. She drew in the shape of the face first, a squarish face with a strong jaw line, and then the thick straight hair that came over the collar at the back. Next, almost without having to think about it, the eyes that were dark and which held a hint of amusement, beneath well shaped dark brows, then a straight, fairly unexceptionable nose. The mouth was the problem—how to give the impression of firmness without hardness, determination without stubbornness. She wet one fingertip and rubbed it lightly on the paper, softening the outline of the mouth and suddenly it was right. She held the paper away from her. It wasn't at all bad, she thought approvingly, and then, laughing at her own foolishness, as good as an Identi-kit picture. She flicked the sketch book shut, packed everything away and stood up, stretching lazily. Where to go now? She was suddenly achingly tired and the thought of a long hot bath was heavenly. Back to the hotel then. She could get a bus almost all the way. But no . . . walking was good for the soul. She would punish herself for the moment's self-indulgence that had just passed.

By the time she was halfway up the Corso, Anne was just about ready to drop, certainly much too tired to make a detour so that she would not have to walk past Luke's apartment. Still, it was hardly likely that anyone would be looking out of the window at that time on a Sunday afternoon and if they were, they would not know her, dressed as she was. As she reached the apartment building she looked steadily at the ground and plodded on.

"Signorina, signorina, please wait!"

Anne halted and looked round. It was Gianetta who had called her name and who was even now running across the wide road to her; Gianetta wearing her Sunday best, a smart fawn linen suit and a little red hat perched on her dark curls.

"Buon giorno, Signorina Anne. I thought it was you. I am with my Mario. He is over there." She turned and waved to a young man who was waiting none too patiently at the wheel of a small Fiat. "I thought perhaps you were going to the apartment, but there is no one there. If you wish to find Signor Patterson, he is in the gardens of the Villa Umberto with Lucy. On Sunday afternoons I go out with Mario to visit his family and Signor Patterson takes Lucy out." She smiled. "He sits in the park and watches Lucy play with the other children. It is easy to find where he is. If you go to the Piazza le Flaminia and turn to the right, there is an entrance there. Do you know it, signorina?"

"Yes."

"Signor Patterson never goes far. There are seats there, and grass for the children." The Italian girl smiled again. "I will say arrivederci for now, signorina."

"Arrivederci," Anne repeated. She watched Gianetta get into the Fiat, whose driver blew impatiently on the horn as he started up the very noisy engine. Then she walked on. Gianetta had taken it for granted that she was going to see Luke and Lucy, and after all, why not? She would not be in Rome that long and when she went home might never see Luke again. The thought was acutely depressing and she determined to see as much of him as possible while she could. Tired feet forgotten, she followed Gianetta's directions and so came to the gardens. Luke was just where Gianetta had said he would be. There were a number of children about with their parents or nurses. Luke was alone, sitting with his arms along the back of the bench, legs crossed, smoking and looking thoughtfully at his daughter. Again it came to Anne that he seemed lonely. She knew it was a stupid thought but she could not dismiss it. There always was something so terribly alone about a widower, even one like Luke who obviously chose to remain in that state. Anne heaved her shoulder bag higher and walked briskly up to him, saying "Good afternoon," in what she hoped was a cheerful voice.

"Hi," Luke said, looking not at all surprised to see her. "I didn't think you'd get my message so soon."

"Your message?" Anne sat on the seat beside him. "I didn't get any message. I met Gianetta and she told me you always come here."

"I phoned your hotel," he explained. "They said you had taken a packed lunch and gone off for the day. I left a message that I'd be here till four and for you to phone me at home after that."

"Oh!" A warm glow of delight stole through Anne so that she was sure he must be able to see it. He had actually wanted her company! She had no idea what to say and it was with relief that she greeted Lucy who had spotted her and come running over. Anne sat down on the grass and played ball with the child, looking, in her tight jeans and with her hair tied back, hardly older than Lucy.

"We've been to the zoo," Lucy told her.

"Have you now? Was it good?"

"Great 'n smashing. There's lions and camels and tigers and crocodiles and. . . ." The list seemed to be never ending. Laughing, Anne looked up and saw that Luke's eyes were fixed on her. He was not smiling and his look was dark and unreadable so that unaccountably she shivered.

"What did you want me for?" she asked a little breathlessly.

"Nothing special. I just wondered what you were doing today, that's all. Where's Tom?"

The question was asked so sharply that she was somewhat confused. Then she said, "Playing golf with your brother." Luke frowned at this. "Apparently Simon asked him last night. They went off this morning, racing away in a damn great sports car."

"A Maserati," Luke said reflectively, his expression relaxing. "Simon always did go in for flashy things . . ." he grinned. "Cars and women!"

"Yes, I can believe that." Anne returned the smile, relieved that whatever had been on his mind to cause the frown had gone. She would like to have asked him if there really was some bone of contention between himself and his brother, but did not like to. After all, it was none of her business. Instead she took off one of her shoes and rubbed her foot. "Oh, my poor feet. I've walked miles today. I've been to the Spanish Steps and the Trevi fountain, and the Colisseum and the Roman Forum. I shall probably be drawing Roman remains in my sleep."

"I heard you telling Monsieur Flambert that you teach art. May I see?"

"Go ahead." She indicated her sketchbook and he picked it up and was already looking at one of the quick sketches she had made the previous day at Saint Peter's before she remembered about the sketch she had made of him. Oh, well, it was too late to do anything about it now. She could hardly snatch the book away from him. She stood up casually and walked over to Lucy, crouching beside the child and talking to her while Luke looked through the sketches.

He was impressed. The drawings were unpolished and often rough and hasty, but there was a vigorous aliveness about them, so that one could almost feel the rough stone or smooth marble. He was surprised and pleased to find that she was so talented. When he came to the final sketch of his own face it took a second or two for him to realize who it was. Not because it was a poor likeness but because people generally don't recognize themselves in such circumstances. He wondered why she had drawn it and couldn't quite decide whether or not the reasons he gave himself were the right ones. That didn't matter much anyway. He closed the sketchbook and stood up, and both Anne and Lucy looked up at him. Anne's face was faintly defiant, almost daring him to make some remark about the sketch of himself. He reached down for Lucy and she slipped her hand into his. He said easily, "Let's go home," and Anne straightened slowly. "Me too?"

"You too."

Lucy's other hand slid into Anne's and they walked back along the path to the Piazza and then along the corso to "home." Lucy chattered happily and occasionally the two adults smiled at each other over her head. Once indoors there was Lucy to be looked after and given tea, for all the staff had Sunday afternoon off, and only momentarily were Luke and Anne left alone, when Lucy went along to her nursery to fetch her dolls, as she said, for tea. In those two or three minutes Luke moved swiftly. He caught Anne by her wrists and led her to the window that overlooked the courtyard. He gazed long into her face and said, sharply, "Are you sure you're really twenty-four?"

Anne laughed. "Positive. Do you want to see my passport?"

"I'll take your word for it. I don't want to be accused of cradle snatching." He smiled tenderly at her. "I think you must be a witch, with that red-gold hair of yours, and green eyes too. Did you only come marching in here yesterday?"

"Yes."

"I feel as though I've known you all my life." Just briefly his fingers touched her face. She knew that another moment and he would kiss her, and also that she wanted him to do just that. More than anything else did she want to be pulled into his arms and kissed until she knew nothing but his mouth and his arms and the hardness of his body against hers. . . .

"I've got all my dollies. We can have tea now." Lucy came in, arms filled with assorted dolls, and Luke drew away from Anne, smiling so tenderly at her that it was as though he really had kissed her, touching her with a warm summer breeze.

Anne remained at the apartment for only a short time. Luke told her he had a dinner appointment that evening, a return invitation from Monsieur and Madame Flambert, and on the morrow he would, of course, be back in his office in the city after the weekend. When Gianetta came in at five, Luke asked her to keep an eye on Lucy for a short while while he drove Anne back to her hotel. Nothing more of an intimate nature had passed between them but Anne didn't mind that. She was quite content that things should slow up a little, not wishing to go headlong into a thing that was hasty and that might burn out as quickly as it had begun. Sitting there beside Luke in the big comfortable car, she felt very happy. Yet she could not resist asking him, "Has Elise Carr been invited to dinner tonight as well?"

He glanced briefly at her before returning his gaze to the road. "Yes. Do you mind?"

"Why should I?"

He shrugged. "There's no reason why you should. Elise is a very beautiful woman but there's nothing between us."

Anne had the feeling that he had intended adding the word "now," and being a woman she had to ask, "Was there once?"

"Yes and no."

"What does that mean?" Anne asked, smiling.

Frankly he said, "Physically yes, emotionally no. It would be difficult for anyone to form a real emotional relationship with Elise. She's a little like a female spider—the sort that eats its mate!" He laughed. "She and Laura loathed each other. I often thought only a very thin veneer of civilization stopped them clawing each other's eyes out!" He pulled the big car to a halt outside the Hotel Tiber and turned to look at Anne. "But then, Elise and Laura were two of a kind."

"Really? I wouldn't have thought so." Anne sounded a little cold and Luke smiled. "You needn't spring to Laura's defense, you know. I don't think you could have known her all that well."

"That's a strange thing to say. She was my sister. Of course I knew her."

"She was my wife," Luke said softly. "And I can assure you, Laura was not all sweetness and light." He put out one hand and rested the fingers lightly on her mouth. "Stop pouting. You look like a sulky schoolgirl."

Anne jerked away from his touch which seemed to

burn her lips. "I'm surprised you waste your precious time on me since you obviously think me so infantile," she said stiffly.

"Oh, Anne, don't tempt me to . . ." he halted, laughing. He got out of the car and walked round to open the door for her.

"I'll call you tomorrow round about seven. Ciao, cara mia."

"What does that mean?" Anne demanded.

"I'll tell you that tomorrow evening."

Anne had a quick shower and got ready for dinner. While she was combing her hair, Tom knocked at the door.

"Can I come in? I've got something to tell you."

"I suppose so. But leave the door open."

"Why? What do you think I'm going to do?" he grinned, but Anne was in no mood for his humor.

"How was the golf?" she asked shortly.

"Great!" Tom sat on the bed and nodded reflectively. "That Simon Patterson sure knows how to live. I don't know whether he has the same kind of money his brother has but he certainly spends as though he has. And he knows some very glamorous females."

"Really?" Anne murmured without much interest.

"You'll never believe it but who should he bring along for his own partner but Elise Carr. Seems like they're quite pally—they were all over each other anyway. I wonder what big brother would say about that."

"Not much probably," Anne commented. "I don't imagine it would bother him at all."

"Hmmm. Maybe not. Still, Patterson doesn't strike me as the sort of bloke to sit back and let his brother walk off with his woman."

"Who was your partner?" Anne asked, changing the subject before it could get too involved or too personal.

"An American girl Elise brought along. Sara Downes, she's called. She had a small part in Elise's last film."

"Who won the golf?"

"Simon and Elise did. But anyway, that wasn't what I wanted to talk about. The thing is, after we had lunch at the clubhouse, the girls disappeared and then Simon and I had a very interesting chat, about big brother Luke . . . and about your sister."

"Oh?" Anne said warily. She had been applying lipstick and now her hand jerked, smudging it. She rubbed it off with a tissue and started again. "And?" she said.

"It seems Simon knew your sister well. They were quite friendly. I gather Laura liked a good time and didn't go much on the settled family life that Luke wanted, having kids and that. She got bored because Luke used to be forever out of Rome on business all over Europe. She used to talk to Simon, who worked in the Rome office at that time, about

Luke, and how jealous he was. If another man even looked at her, which apparently they often did because she was a real looker, Luke used to go through the roof. He has a hell of a temper."

Anne looked quickly at him. "I don't believe all that. What a load of rubbish. Oh, I agree with what you've said about Laura. But she wasn't a fool. She wouldn't risk losing him, apart from his money . . . well, it's not as though she would have married him just for that, not Luke."

"Yeah, well, you're slightly prejudiced on that score, aren't you? I suppose you think Laura must have been crazily in love with Luke. From what I've been hearing about Laura she was never crazily in love with anyone, except maybe herself. You don't know much about life, do you, Anne? Ever heard the saying that the worst sin is being found out?"

"You'll be telling me next that Luke did find out . . . whatever it is you're hinting at . . . that Laura was having an affair presumably . . . and killed her because of it."

"It's happened," Tom said dryly. "And what I think is, she was having an affair all right, with Simon, and Luke found out. Can you imagine how Luke would react if he discovered his wife was having an affair with his brother? In case you hadn't noticed, there's no love lost between them."

"That's stupid!" Anne snapped. "The letter says Laura was going to tell Luke. Why should she tell him that?"

"Maybe she thought he'd find out and decided to

get in first. Do the repentant little woman bit. It's worked on harder, tougher men than Luke Patterson. She wrote you the letter because she was still scared of what his reaction would be."

Anne stood up, smoothed down her dress and glared at Tom. "Listen, you are being ridiculous! Luke didn't kill Laura. It was an accident. Luke is a civilized man. He doesn't have that kind of temper, I'm sure. And he talks about Laura. If you kill someone you don't talk about them, or have their portrait hanging on the wall."

"You do if you want people to think everything was all right between you."

"Oh . . . Tom!" Anne cried exasperated. She stepped out of the room, herding him out and slamming the door behind them. "I don't want to talk about it. You're welcome to your stupid ideas but *I* don't want to know."

"If he did kill your sister, wouldn't you want him to be punished?" Tom asked.

"As he didn't kill her, that question doesn't arise. I said I didn't want to talk about it. If you persist, I shall sit at another table."

Tom sighed, and desisted.

Six

On Monday morning when Anne awoke, it was to find that the weather had changed drastically. The rain crashed against her window and the temperature had dropped several degrees. She pulled up her shutters and looked out on a cold, rain washed Via Flaminia; it was enough to make anyone depressed, but nothing could really depress her that day. For Luke had called her "cara mia" which she knew must be some form of endearment, and tonight she would see him. Tom's suggestions and hints went over her head. She understood why he was interested but was not herself concerned. If Laura had been having an affair with Simon, then she had been a fool. Anne did not remember Laura as being a fool—selfish maybe, and willful, but not foolish. Though perhaps, as Luke had implied, she had not known her sister very well.

"I thought I might do some shopping," she told Tom. "I expect I can find some shops a little more within the range of my pocket than those in the Via

Veneto and I suppose I'd better get some presents to take home. Do you want to come?"

"Shopping? No thank you. I've got to meet someone," Tom replied in dark mystery. Anne gave him a straight look.

"Not Simon again?"

"That's right. Why not? He's a very interesting guy."

"He ought to be shot, spreading rumors about his own brother and, for that matter, about my sister. I have a good mind to tell Luke just what he's been saying."

"Don't you dare!"

"Oh, I won't." There would be more important things to say, Anne thought, smiling to herself.

By the time Tom went out, it was raining so hard that Anne decided not to venture out at all. She sat in the small comfortable lounge reading and sketching, passing the time by doing a series of little sketches of Lucy, and then of the hotel staff as they went about their work: the maids who came to clean the lounge, the dark-eyed waiter who brought her mid-morning coffee, the two large chamber maids with arms full of fresh laundry, the swarthy, paunchy restaurant manager. When, intrigued by what she was doing, one of the waiters saw her sketches, there were many exclamations of delight and now it seemed to Anne that everyone working in the hotel took the opportunity of pausing in the lounge to examine her work. Solemnly she tore off the various drawings and presented them to those portrayed. A second cup of coffee that she ordered was accompanied by a large, fattening but delicious piece of chocolate gateaux and a beaming smile from Guiseppe, the waiter. Anne had the feeling the gateaux would not appear on her bill. It occurred to her that she would get very good service from now on, and this surmise proved to be correct at lunchtime, a meal she ate alone, for Tom did not return. There seemed always to be at least two waiters hovering and she never had to wait longer than a minute or two between courses.

"Signorina," Guiseppe said, when he brought her fresh fruit salad and ice cream, "I wonder if I might ask ... mia madre, she is very old and lives in Milano. I should like so much to have a picture to send her. You understand, she is quite alone and . . . ."

Anne smiled. "I should be delighted to sketch you, Guiseppe. But please, don't say anything to anyone else. I am here to see Rome and can't spend all my time doing commissions."

His black eyes sparkled with delight at the conspiracy and his voice dropped. "But of course, signorina. I will say no word about it. Grazie, signorina."

Anne stayed in the lounge for a while letting the huge lunch go down. By then a thin watery sun had managed to break through the thick cloud and she thought she would go for a walk.

She went swiftly to her room to fetch a jacket and her camera and sketch book. Going through the foyer she met the friendly Guiseppe again.

"You are going out, signorina?"

"Just for a short walk. I thought I would go to the Castel Sant'Angelo. It doesn't seem to be too far and it will give me a chance to see the Tiber."

"Ah, yes, signorina, and on the Ponte Sant'Angelo there are many fine statues that you will no doubt like to draw." He smiled broadly as he wished her "ciao," an Italian word that Anne had learnt could mean "hello," "good-bye," as well as a host of other things.

The Tiber, she decided, was not the romantic river that the name conjured up. The tide was out and banks of grey, dirty mud were piled high on either side and the river water looked very murky. She crossed the river at the Ponte Sant'Angelo, duly admiring the tall statues of angels that stood at intervals along both sides of the bridge. Directly before her was the Castel Sant'Angelo which she had last seen from the summit of Saint Peter's. The castle was also the mausoleum of Hadrian; it was a huge place with a circular tower of red brick and massive fortifications. Anne was not in the mood for sketching and besides, there was a fairly stiff wind that would have made this difficult, so she contented herself with taking photographs instead. She was just debating whether to take the opportunity of venturing into the castle and viewing the treasures that her guidebook told her it guarded when, with a screech of brakes a silver-grey Cadillac pulled up beside her and she saw Luke at the wheel.

The sudden, unexpected sight of him caused her heart to leap. She saw, when he got out of the car and moved around to open the door for her, that he was today dressed very much as the businessman, in a grey three-piece suit. The suit was superbly cut in a fairly modern style with longish, slightly fitted jacket and flared trousers with razor sharp creases. Across the front of his waistcoat shone the gleam of a gold watch chain. Such an obviously expensive suit would have looked well on any man, but to Anne's admiring eyes, Luke looked wonderful.

"You look very distinguished," she said, smiling quickly. The smile faded, stiffening on her face, when she looked up into his eyes. She had seen them stern, tender, teasing, laughing, but not like this, not hard and cold. Uncertainly, she slid into the passenger seat and he slammed the door behind her. So far he had said nothing. She watched him walk round the front of the car and get in beside her. He did not look at her but started up the engine with an unnecessary roar that seemed to be echoed by the thudding of her heart. Anne struggled to remain calm. Perhaps he had had a difficult morning at work. She said quickly, she hoped gaily, "Was it coincidence that you found me there?"

"No." He spoke shortly, as though he had no real wish to speak.

"Then how . . .?"

"They told me at your hotel."

"Oh!"

Thereafter, nothing was said. In a moment Luke had drawn the car up outside his apartment. His chauffeur, looking very unhappy, stood on the pavement, rather as though he had been dumped there. Now Luke snapped something at him in Italian and he got into the Cadillac and drove it away. Luke took Anne's arm, his fingers digging in just above the elbow, almost dragging her inside. He called the elevator and when it did not come, swore fiercely and started up the stairs. It was then that Anne tried to show a little independence. She dragged her arm from his hand, saying, "I can manage perfectly well, thank you." He didn't even stop climbing. He opened the door to his home and stood back so that Anne could enter in front of him. "Come into my parlor," said the spider to the fly, Anne thought to herself, trying to rid herself of her sense of foreboding with a little humor. She glanced up at Luke's impassive face; if it were possible, anger made him better-looking than ever. She found herself thinking that he looked like a devil, the way she had always imagined John Milton's Lucifer, a tall, blonde devil with cold, granite-like eyes, not ugly but beautiful.

The apartment was in silence; there was no Lucy coming running to meet them, no calm-faced Gina, smiling Gianetta, no sounds of industry from the kitchen. Anne preceded Luke into the room where he had first taken her, saying lightly, "Where is everyone?"

"Out!" he said shortly. "I didn't particularly want anyone to hear what I have to say to you."

She turned to face him then, as he stood with his back to the door. His eyes raked her slender figure in its cream linen dress and jacket, the long slim legs which he had admired from the beginning, and her feet neatly shod in dark blue leather sling-backs. He looked slowly up at her face, framed by that glorious red-gold hair, the sort of hair that any man might long to run his fingers through. She was looking puzzled, scared, slightly defiant; it was a touching look, reminding him as it did of Lucy on the few occasions when he had spoken sharply to her—bewilderment that this glorious, omnipotent being who was her father could ever raise his voice to her. It was a look he would have found endearing except that he knew how false it was. Just one more instance of how clever she was. He could feel the anger building up inside him and made no attempt to stop it; anger was better than pain.

"You really had me fooled," he said slowly, continuing to look at her up and down in such a way that she flushed uncomfortably. "Me! Fooled by a little slip of a thing I could break in half with my bare hands."

"Luke, I don't know what . . ." she began to say, but he interrupted, his voice harsh. "Be quiet! You can have your say afterwards, when I've finished. If you still think you have anything to say. I thought I knew all the angles. I can handle sophisticates, women who throw their bodies at me. But you . . . the well brought-up, well scrubbed, English school-girl type, man, that was a new one. And to think that I very nearly fell for it. But you are hoist with your own petard, my dear. You should have put a curb on that runaway pen of your mother's."

"What are you talking about?" Anne demanded, finding her voice at last. She felt as though she had been flayed; any minute now and her knees would give way beneath her, or she would cry. The thought of crying in front of him was too much to bear.

Luke pulled from his inside pocket an airmail envelope and even from where she stood Anne recognized her mother's agitated handwriting. "I had a letter," he said softly. "It came this morning and I've spent all the time since then wondering how I came to be such a bloody fool as to believe in your . . . act."

"It wasn't an act."

He ignored this. "Your mother jumped the gun a little. She writes that she feels there needn't be a tug of war battle over Lucy. If I just hand her over to you, instead of you having to snatch her, things will be so much pleasanter." He laughed suddenly, harshly, without mirth. "If I just hand over my daughter . . . ."

Anne spoke. "Oh, God," she whispered, and then,

"You don't understand anything! I can explain that letter to you—and my mother's state of mind. She doesn't mean the things she writes. If you'd only let her see her granddaughter . . . she has the right to . . . ."

"She has no rights!" he thundered. "You have no rights! Christ Almighty, Lucy is my daughter! Your sister is dead, and when she died Lucy became my sole responsibility. Do you think I would let her fall into the clutches of a woman who writes letters like this? Or someone like you, you little bitch!"

"Don't you start calling me names!" Anne cried back, beside herself now with anger at the injustice of this attack. "You're pig-headed and bigoted and . . . and so stupid! If you think that I would want to snatch Lucy away from you, then you know nothing about people, absolutely nothing, for all that you think you're so damn clever. I wanted to see Lucy, of course I did, but it doesn't take brains to see that she's happy and loved. And what's more we have got rights, human rights, to see a child who is our flesh and blood. My God, we would even have accepted you, you stupid man! But no, I suppose you thought you were too good for us, the great Luke Patterson. Well, as far as I'm concerned, you can stay here in your luxury apartment till you rot, and I hope your money chokes you!"

She ran to the door, pushing blindly past him, tears streaming down her face, wanting only to get out, to run and run, and put as much distance between herself and him as possible. The front door defeated her. It had an unfamiliar lock and through her tears she could not see it properly and stood there fumbling and sobbing.

Luke reached her. He put one hand over both hers as they were on the door fastening, so that she became suddenly still. He said, his voice different, strange, uncertain, "Anne?" and then, when she didn't—couldn't—answer, "I'm sorry."

She still could say nothing. She looked up at him, hardly seeing him through her tears. She knew she should get away but it was as though her body was boneless, without substance; she had neither the will nor the ability to move away. He took his hand from hers and put it on her shoulder, turning her to face him, and then, with a jerk, she was pulled against him and his arms were about her so tightly that she could hardly breathe, her face pressed into the thick, soft material of his jacket front. He stood still, holding her, head bent so that his cheek was against her hair.

"I'm sorry," he repeated after a very long time.

Her eyes were tight closed, her face still pressed against his shoulder, her arms tight round his waist. She could feel the urgency in his hard, powerful grasp, the tautness of his body. After what seemed an eternity, when her own heart had stilled to a pace that was almost normal, she was gently eased off his shoulder and they looked at each other. He took a crisp white handkerchief from his top pocket and gently wiped away the remaining tears from her cheeks; almost without thought she smiled tremulously.

As though the smile released him Luke tipped her chin up and kissed her softly on the lips. Anne's hands slid up over the lapels of his jacket and lightly her fingers touched the hair at the back of his neck. He felt the movement and stiffened, and then once more she was dragged against him, the kiss deepening, her mouth opening beneath his. In all her wildest imaginings Anne had never dreamed a kiss could be thus; filled with delight she clung round his neck, her eyes tightly closed as she seemed to drown with sensation.

Somehow, though she never knew how, they got back into the saloon. When Anne "came round" so that for a moment she was able almost to think straight, she was sitting on the settee, Luke's arm across her shoulders, his other hand holding both hers tightly. They smiled at each other, she shyly, he with something like wonder.

"What happened?" she murmured. "One minute I was being yelled at, the next minute . . . ."

"Hush," he said. "Don't talk. Let me look at you."

"Why?"

"Why? Don't fish for compliments. Because you are lovely and well-worth looking at. Your eyes are sparkling, little Anne, and your mouth is a delicious pink."

"Lipstick."

"Rubbish. There's not a scrap of lipstick left." He

covered her mouth again with his and laughed softly when he moved back. "You kiss as though you've never been kissed before."

"Well, I have."

"I should think so. English men aren't that thick."

Anne smiled. "I've never been kissed that way before," she admitted.

"I'm glad of that," he teased gently. "That's not the way to kiss a . . . ."

"Well brought-up, well scrubbed English school-girl," Anne supplied with a smile. She pressed one hand against his lips. "Don't say it! I shouldn't have brought that up—not now. I think we must have explanations, Luke, but not for the moment."

"Definitely not for the moment," he agreed and there was a long, long silence between them. This time when he raised his head, he said, "You're beginning to learn, my darling."

"Am I?"

"There are so many things I'd like to teach you."

Anne chuckled; she rested her head against his arm, her long hair across the back of the settee and over his shoulder. "I bet!"

He grinned. "Not so innocent after all."

"Innocent—but not naïve."

"Let's say, unawakened."

"Maybe. Luke, I'm not that young. I can't help the way I look. Don't treat me like a child."

"Am I doing that? I don't normally treat children this way."

"Oh, you! You know what I mean." She touched

the silver and blue tie he wore, now loosened. "Luke, you don't really think I wanted to . . . to snatch Lucy from you?"

"Of course I don't. I lost my head. I was a bloody fool."

"I wouldn't do anything to hurt Lucy. I love her."

"You," he teased. "You're so soft-hearted you'd love anyone."

Slowly, delighted but overwhelmed by the familiarity, Anne ran one hand over his hair, letting her fingers dig into the thickness of it. "I love you," she said softly.

He caught at her hand, pressing his mouth against the palm. "After what I said to you, I don't deserve that."

"What you said was . . . natural. I don't blame you even if you did jump to hasty conclusions. I know my mother has written you some odd letters but . . . ."

"It doesn't matter, my love."

"It does! Don't you see, Luke? She's my mother. If she had no excuse, then it would be different." She sat up sharply, taking both his hands in hers. "Let me tell you about it, please."

"All right, darling. Listen, I could do with some strong black coffee to cool me down a bit. Go into the kitchen and switch on the percolator—I expect Signora Verdi left it all ready—while I get changed. I feel like I'm in a strait jacket in this outfit."

The kitchen was marvellous, Anne thought. Having switched on the electric coffee percolator, she explored the many cupboards and fitted units, the infrared cooker, the eye-level oven, all the other gadgets; she had no idea as to the purpose of some of these labor-saving devices. Everything was stainless steel or gleaming Italian marble. It would be a dream of a kitchen to cook in, she thought, taking a sniff from one of the many wooden topped jars of spices and herbs. She sat at the formica topped table, resting her elbows upon it and, chin cupped in hands, thought about what had been happening in the last half-hour. Everything in her life had changed; nothing would ever be the same again.

Luke came in, dressed in tan colored slacks and a brown cotton shirt. He switched off the percolator and fetched large coffee mugs and brown sugar, and cream from the ice box.

"Wake up, dreamer," he said, dropping a kiss on the top of Anne's head. She laughed and looked up, receiving another kiss this time on the lips. Luke pulled out a chair and sat beside her; he lit cigarettes for them both and Anne poured coffee.

"The letter," she said, drawing on her cigarette. "Can I see it, please?"

"If you really want to." He put the letter in front of her and she read it swiftly, sighing heavily.

"Oh, dear. Were they all like this?"

"No. That one just about tops the lot."

Anne stirred her coffee; her hair fell forward on either side of her face and unlike that last time, when Luke had merely looked at that fine ridge of hairs that ran from the back of her neck down her spine, he now put out one hand and gently touched the soft skin with the tips of his fingers. He felt her skin tremble at the light touch. He rested the palm of his hand on her neck, cupping it gently and she moved against his hand like a cat.

"She isn't really like that," Anne began uncertainly. "I mean, she's perfectly all right most of the time, honestly she is. It's just that she has terrible depressions. I've gathered from my grandparents that she was always highly strung and what happened to Dad was just too much for her, as it would be too much for most women. Then Laura being killed—she just cracked up again. She was in hospital for ages having treatment and really, she's mostly all right now."

She halted to take a sip of coffee and Luke, his hand still on her neck, sensing that the contact helped her, asked, "What did happen to your father?"

Anne looked up, startled. "Don't you know? Didn't Laura ever tell you?" He shook his head. "Oh, God!" she cried. "How could she not . . . ."

"Laura didn't talk much about her family," he said gently.

"No." Anne took a deep breath and looked straight at him. After all these years she still hated to think about it, and she loathed people's reactions when they heard. They either withdrew with horror and disgust, or were sympathetic. She had never been able to decide which was worse. "He embezzled a large sum of money, thousands of pounds. We never knew, of course. We just thought he was lucky on the stock market. I was about sixteen then and Laura was living at home. One day I got back from school and there was a police car outside our house—some CID men. Dad disappeared. He must have realized he had been found out. He went off and booked himself into a horrible little hotel in the East End." She halted. "Can I have another cigarette please?"

Wordlessly he pushed the packet towards her, his eyes never leaving her face. Suddenly she didn't look sixteen, or even eighteen. She looked very much an adult, mature woman and he had never realized it was possible to love anyone so much.

"He hanged himself," she said conversationally. She glanced quickly at Luke. He was watching her but the look in his eyes reflected neither horror nor sympathy, but something entirely different, a warm glow of loving that somehow robbed the story she had just told of most of its hurt. She said sharply, "Why didn't Laura tell you? She should have."

"Anne, I honestly don't think you knew much about Laura. Laura loved—Laura. When she left her family I don't believe she gave any of you more than the odd passing thought." She flinched miserably. "I'm sorry, my love, but it's true."

It was strange that he had used almost the same expression Tom had used about Laura. "Laura loved Laura." Tom had discovered this truth by talking to Simon about her. "I know," Anne said sadly. "I think I always knew really, when she left England at once, after Dad's death, so that she wouldn't have any of the nastiness rubbing off on to her. She never even stayed for his funeral. We heard that she had married several months later . . . oh, it isn't you I'm blaming, Luke. Nor even Laura really. I suppose she couldn't help being like that. After Dad died, Mum had a nervous breakdown and tried to kill herself. It was ages before she even knew what Laura had done. When she did, she was terribly hurt. You see Laura was so beautiful and clever and gay that she was sort of special. Mum finally got over her desertion a bit and even started boasting about Laura and her rich husband. She imagined Laura would visit us, all decked out in furs and dripping with diamonds! When she didn't, that upset Mum too. Then, when we passed through Rome on holiday, she hoped to see you both, and you were in . . .?"

"Greece," he offered quietly. He remembered the occasion vividly even though it was over six years ago. He could see Laura pacing up and down the lounge, the letter from her mother in her long nervous fingers; she was about four months pregnant then with a child she lost just a month or so later, and that hadn't exactly improved her temper. She hated the thought of her thickening waistline.

"They're coming here," she had cried. "Here to Rome, in July. They're on one of those beastly cheap package holidays. They want to meet you."

"That's fine," Luke said. "Why not?"

"Why not? Because . . . because I don't want to see them, that's why not. I've finished with my family. Oh, Luke, they're awful. There's mother, a bag of nerves and neurotic, and my grandparents are coming with her and they're so old-fashioned and fussy. And Anne . . . ."

"Well? What can be wrong with Anne?" he inquired sarcastically.

"Nothing. She's all right."

Luke could now see why Anne had been "all right." It was because Anne had adored Laura. That was just what Laura liked. She had been determined not to be in Rome when her family passed through. He could, she said, go away somewhere on business, and she would write that it was just unfortunate that they wouldn't be in Rome then. He had finally given in, partly because it was so much easier to give in to Laura, partly because he didn't want her getting into one of her thankfully rare bouts of screaming hysteria, not while she was pregnant, and mostly because at that time he had been still very much under her spell. He had thought then that it was love—certainly he had wanted her. She had shown a prowess in bed that had at first startled and even annoyed him. Like most men he would have preferred to lead the way in that particular aspect of their married life. But he was still blindly lost under the force of her fascination. He realized now that what he had felt for Laura was nothing to do with love. He had found that out a long time ago, but it was made all the more clear to him from the moment that Anne had walked, unasked, uninvited and certainly unwanted, into his life.

"Luke?" Anne said uncertainly, and he came out of his daydream and smiled at her.

"Sorry. I was just thinking about you . . . and Laura. Go on with your story."

"There's not much more to tell. Laura's death was just one more blow for mother. She had another breakdown. When she was better Gran and Grandad took her in and helped her. We didn't know at first that she had started this yearning to get at Lucy. I don't know how long she had been writing to you before we found out. We tried to stop it but she got so upset—she seems to regard Lucy as a replacement for Laura."

Luke looked ashamed. "I wish one of you had let me know how things were," he said. "I didn't keep Lucy away from you because of pure selfishness. In fact I did think of taking her to England when she was a little older. Then I started getting these letters from your mother and . . . I guess they got my back up. If I had only realized . . . ."

"We didn't know you, Luke! I did think of writing once but I used to get a bit annoyed with you myself." She smiled to rob the words of their sting. "We didn't know anything about you at all except that you were very well off. Laura let us know that much all right."

His hand was still on her neck, warm and comforting against her skin. She looked at him, longing and love in her eyes. "You aren't a bit like I imagined you'd be."

"Oh? What did you imagine?"

"I don't know . . . someone older perhaps. Not someone looking like . . . ." She stopped talking and let out an involuntary giggle. Luke was relieved to see that her sombre story had in no way left its mark upon her, but also intrigued.

"Go on. Looking like what?"

"Gina thinks—and I'm rather inclined to agree with her—that you look like Robert Redford."

He had the grace to redden in embarrassment so that she let out a snort of smothered laughter and stood up as he grabbed at her. "You little cat. Wait till I get my hands on you!"

Anne fled, laughing, out of the kitchen. He caught her halfway down the hall, tickling her unmercifully until she begged him to stop. He wrapped his arms round her, holding her tight so that she could not escape. Anne was weak with laughter. "Oh, don't, Luke. I can't stand it. I'll have hysterics."

"Serves you right if you do. You realize you're completely at my mercy, don't you? These apartments are soundproofed and you could scream and scream and no one would hear you."

"I wouldn't scream," she smiled and lifted her face to be kissed. She was kissed until her brain whirled and her lips were sore, and then, abruptly, she was released. He went into the saloon, picked up her jacket and tossed it to her.

"Put that on. I'm taking you back to your hotel."

"Why?"

"Two reasons. I have to get changed for one. I'm meeting a business colleague at four-thirty and later having dinner with him and his wife at the Hilton."

"Oh, damn you!" she said rudely. "You said two reasons."

He looked levelly at her from across the room, wondering whether to tell the truth. "Because if you stay here any longer, I shan't be able to keep my hands off you," he said softly.

When she still made no move, he added, "I mean it, Anne. I'm no saint and I don't pretend to be. Everything in me is yelling that I should take you off to bed right now. So put on your jacket and I'll take you home, there's a good girl."

"I'm not a child, Luke, I've told you that before."

He took her face gently between his hands. "Darling, I know you're not. You're a lovely, desirable woman and, by God, I want you very much! But not this way. Not a quick scuffle on the bed, which is all it would be. When I make love to you, it's going to be real and forever. Understand?"

"Not entirely," she smiled. "But I'll think about it."

Seven

With a promise that he would pick her up the following evening at seven, and a swift, sweet kiss on the cheek, Luke left Anne on the pavement outside the Hotel Tiber. Bemused and in a kind of dream, she went gliding up in the lift to the seventh floor and her room. When she glimpsed herself in the mirror she was heartily relieved that she had not met anyone in reception when she had slipped in to get her key. Her hair was all over the place, her eyes were alight with ill suppressed excitement, her cheeks were flushed and her lips red and slightly swollen. She touched them gently, smiling secretly at her reflection. I'm in love, she thought in wonder, in love, in love, in love. She slipped out of the very crumpled dress and lay down on her bed, her eyes closed so that she could think about him better, and relived every moment, every word spoken, every expression that had passed since he had picked her up outside the Castel Sant'Angelo. Even the terrible things he had accused her of she remembered because the pain was bittersweet, knowing what was to follow. And surely the sweetest of all was what had last passed between them. She knew with a firm certainty that she would have gone willingly to bed with him, without thought or excuse. She also knew that she would have, if not regretted it, been a little sorry about it. That would seem an old-fashioned notion to many girls of her age but it merely reflected her own values and the values she had been brought up to believe in. She recognized her own desires; stupid to pretend she did not want him physically as well as emotionally, but knew that to have given in so early in their relationship to those desires might have tarnished something precious and wonderful. How much more difficult it must have been for Luke to take the initiative in fighting against his own physical needs? He was a virile, very masculine man who had no doubt known and loved many women. Yet he had said—what were his words? "When I make love to you, it's going to be real and forever." What a wonderful thought, Anne sighed.

She dozed happily for a while before getting up, showering and preparing for dinner. By the time she had washed and dried her hair, put on a clean fresh blouse and skirt and applied make-up carefully, she looked, she considered, reasonably calm. Calm enough anyway to go downstairs to meet Tom in the bar. But she could not disguise the sparkle in her eyes, or her own laughter that kept bubbling over.

"What the hell's the matter with you?" Tom asked disgruntled. His day had been far from successful. First he had got soaked to the skin waiting for Simon to turn up. Then the American had been two hours late. Finally he had taken Tom to meet some friends of his in a very dingy sort of bar somewhere in the center of Rome. The friends had been playing poker. Hoping that by remaining with Simon he might learn something else about Luke, and also fancying himself as something of a poker player, Tom had stayed on. By three in the afternoon, his head ached with a combination of the thick, smoke-filled atmosphere, the wine he had been drinking, and the fact that he had lost a good deal more than he could afford. The sight of Anne, all pink and white and glowing, the most obvious picture of a girl in love that he had ever seen, did not improve his temper. He wasn't vindictive in the normal way but he was fed up and in the mood to shatter anyone's dreams.

"Been cavorting with your sister's murderer?" he inquired conversationally. Anne stared at him, the color fading in her cheeks and the sparkle from her eyes. She stood up and walked away to sit on her own. Tom watched her, immediately contrite, and after a moment followed her.

"Sorry. I don't know why I said that. It was a stupid thing to say."

"It certainly was."

"I've had a terrible day."

"You look it. I've had a wonderful day."

"Ask him about the letter, did you?"

"What?"

"The letter from your sister. Have you still got it?"

"Of course I have."

"And have you asked him about it?"

"No."

"It's what brought you to Rome, Anne. You were full of it when we met on the plane."

"Yes, but I hadn't met Luke then."

Tom leaned forward and quoted softly, "I've decided to tell Luke. He has a terrible temper and I'm sure he'll kill me."

"I don't want to hear."

"Okay. I won't say anymore. But do two things for me, and for yourself. Don't forget the letter—it doesn't cease to exist just because your head is up in the clouds. And come with me tonight to meet Simon and hear what he has to say."

"No! I certainly don't intend to listen to his poison."

"Anne, don't be an ostrich. No matter what you think, Laura was frightened of Luke, and she had some terrible secret that she thought was so bad that he might kill her if he found out. It's in black and white and you can't deny it."

"People say things. Haven't you ever said 'I'll kill you' to someone? It doesn't mean you literally will."

"I think you owe it to your sister to find the truth."

"I owe nothing to Laura. Nothing! She didn't care for us when she was alive. Why should I care for her now she's dead? No, Tom, that's no reason."

He had his final argument ready. If it didn't sway her, he would give up, he told himself. He would call it quits. "You know what I think, Anne? I think you're scared. You're scared because you think it might be true, that he did kill Laura. If you really didn't believe it, you would laugh at what I've said, and you'd be perfectly willing to hear what Simon has to say. You're chicken, girl, that's what. Why, you won't even show Luke that letter because you're frightened he won't have a reasonable explanation."

It would work. He knew it. Strange how even the most intelligent people became children when it came to such an argument. No one likes being called "chicken."

Anne stiffened and glared at him, part of her mind knowing that Tom was manipulating her with a rotten argument, but she had to prove to him that his ideas were nonsense.

"All right," she quietly agreed. "I'll come with you to meet your precious Simon."

The place that Tom took her to was near the Pantheon. They had to walk past this strange, rotund building with its eight massive pillars supporting the triangular facade and Anne, partly to put off the approaching meeting, stopped to look more closely at the dedication to Agrippa that was inscribed in large letters above the pillars. Tom tugged at her arm and she walked with him down a number of narrow, dark streets, many cobbled, until they reached a small doorway. This led into a dimly lit bar. It was no tourist place, Anne saw at a glance. The men who sat about drinking wine were Romans, and they eyed Anne's slim figure with interest; she heard soft comments being made, obviously about her, so that she flushed with embarrassment and was glad she did not speak Italian. She grabbed Tom's arm as he threaded his way through the tables to the back of the bar, muttering, "This is an awful place, Tom. I wish I hadn't come."

To be truthful, Tom was wishing he hadn't brought her. It hadn't seemed so bad before, but now he began to see through her eyes the dim lighting, the dirty tablecloths, the greasy floor, and the blatant, lascivious eyes of the men who watched her. He put an arm across her shoulder, as though to point out to the Italians that she was spoken for, but this gesture merely provoked soft laughter from them.

At a table at the rear of the bar Simon Patterson sat over a carafe of red wine. A girl was sitting close beside him, a well-built Italian girl, dark-eyed and attractive in an over-ripe way, locked closely in Simon's embrace. Seeing Anne and Tom approach, Simon muttered something to her and she pouted and moved away. Anne stared in astonishment at Simon. On the two occasions she had seen him, he had been very elegant and well-dressed, a typical "young rich man about town." True, she had sensed a certain weakness in him, but that weakness, it seemed to her, would cause him to run towards the very best to be found of everything. The Hotel Grand where he was staying was as far removed from this place as Elise Carr was from the rather dirty if luscious Italian girl. Simon stood up as they came to his table and smiled at Anne, his eyes lingering on the neck of her blouse with its low round neckline that just revealed the beginnings of her breasts. Anne stared with scarcely concealed loathing at him. It was hard to believe that this slovenly looking creature with the unkempt hair and unshaven chin was Luke's half-brother. Or that she had once thought them alike.

Simon was just balancing on the line between being drunk and sober. As Tom ordered drinks for himself and Anne, determinedly not meeting the censure in Anne's eyes, Simon said, "Well, well, the lovely Anne. Don't look so shocked, sweetie. Everyone likes to do a little slumming sometimes."

"Some people might," Anne returned and he laughed.

"You really are like Laura. She didn't care for this place either. Very high class was Laura."

"Really?"

"Sure she was. I reckon maybe you're even better-looking than she was—in a more innocent way. You are bellisima, Anne." He breathed the word, leaning forward so that his face was inches from her own, and Anne smelt the wine on his breath. She recoiled immediately and he saw this; a swift look of real anger crossed his face, changing its good looks to ugliness. He would not, Anne realized, be a nice man to cross. He would make an implacable enemy. She shivered then as she realized that for some reason, he and Luke were enemies. What had happened between the two brothers? Could it be, as Tom suggested, that Laura had been involved?

Tom seemed to notice none of this. "Simon," he said, "tell Anne about your brother."

"My brother!" Simon snarled. "That bastard. The great Luke Patterson. He thinks he's so bloody good, he thinks he can buy anything. Well, he can't buy *me* off. I know what I know. I've got something in here . . . ." He tapped his head. "Man, it's so sweet to have that brother of mine in my power."

"What are you talking about?" Anne demanded. "How have you got Luke in your power?"

"Never mind, beautiful, never mind. One of these days I'll tell what I know. To get back at all the slights I've had to suffer in that bastard's hands. I'll tell you something. I was all set to be given the Rome office. Luke was going back to the States. Then Luke had a word with the old man, and suddenly, wham! Simon was out on his ear. I promised myself there and then that one fine day I'd get back at him, and by Christ, the time is very near."

"Do you think Luke killed Laura?" Tom demanded, feeling that Simon was rambling on about revenge without any real meaning.

Simon shrugged. "She was afraid of him. She told me so. She said that though he was always charming and loving to her in public, that he was very different when they were alone. He was jealous and had violent rages. He used to hit her."

Anne could believe that Luke was a jealous lover. She had the feeling he wasn't a man to go much on Women's Lib. He was one of life's takers and what he had he would not share. There would be no second chances for a woman who was unfaithful to him. Yet she couldn't imagine him resorting to physical violence. That, she was positive, was Simon's bitterness and hatred coming out. Perhaps he thought that the worst thing a man could do to a woman was to knock her about. Anne was sure that mental violence could be far worse.

For the first time she wondered, what if Laura really was having an affair and Luke found out? Or, as Tom suggested, Laura thought he would find out and decided to tell him and "get in first?" Laura was a very modern woman, not exactly promiscuous but Anne knew she had had lovers. She made no secret of this to her young sister, keeping it from her parents only to save the bother that would have resulted if they had known. Would a woman used to picking and choosing, a woman lovely enough to be able to do this, be capable of settling down with one man, even if that man was Luke? Anne could think of nothing more wonderful in the whole world than to be married to Luke, but Laura may have seen things differently.

"If you believe Luke could have killed Laura, why don't you tell the police?" she demanded of Simon.

"Don't be crazy, sweetheart. Who'd believe me? I'm just a crummy kid brother, suffering from jealousy because Luke has done better than me. Besides, like

I said, I've got something far better held over Luke's head. One day I might just use it."

Tom, believing Simon was indulging in pipe dreams with this wild talk of revenge, interrupted the flow. "I've decided something," he said. "I'm going to Capri for a couple of days. I'll try to find out what really happened. Anne, why don't you come too?"

"No thank you," she icily replied. She stood up. "I want to go, Tom."

"But . . . ."

"Now, please."

"Oh, very well." Tom took his leave of Simon who remained seated, eyes half-closed as he dreamed his own twisted thoughts of revenge. Anne shivered as she looked at him. Luke had likened him to a "bad penny" but had he any real idea what was going on in his half-brother's mind? She led the way swiftly out of the unsavory little place and the fresh air smelt wonderful.

"I don't know why you have to get all huffy," Tom complained.

"Then you're more stupid than I thought possible! Can't you see that Simon wants revenge on Luke because of something personal between them? And if you think I'm doing anything to help him get that revenge, you're very much mistaken. Because that's all he wants, Tom. It's obvious if only you'd open your eyes to see. He has this grudge against Luke. I guessed that when I first met him. But there's something else between them too, not just that about Simon losing his job. Perhaps it has to do with Laura, maybe it's something entirely different. But he's using you to help him get his own back. Well, he's not using me." She halted and faced him. "Don't you see that if you get a re-opening of the inquest into Laura's death, Luke is bound to suffer, even though he's innocent? There's no smoke without fire, that's what people will say. And if that happens, Simon will have got his revenge over Luke."

"You really are in love with him, aren't you?" Tom asked.

"Yes, I am. I don't know how it happened in such a short time but it has and I'm not a bit ashamed to admit it. He's a wonderful man, worth a million of that awful smarmy little squirt we just left. He made me feel dirty. I don't think I'll ever forget those awful looks he gave me."

"Don't be so dramatic, Anne. Look, I've got a duty to get to the truth and by God, if I can get at it by going to Capri, then to Capri I'm going!"

Eight

The following morning Tom paid his bill at the Hotel Tiber and went off to get a bus to Naples where he could catch the boat to Capri. Anne watched him go without much regret. She had got to know the staff of the hotel and some of the other guests and anyway was quite happy to be on her own. The weather was still cold and miserable, more like an English spring day than an Italian one, but Anne refused to let this spoil her holiday. She spent the morning with Gianetta and Lucy at the apartment on the Via del Corso, getting to know more about the child and about Luke. He had left word that she was to have the run of the apartment and while Gianetta gave Lucy her mid-morning milk, Anne explored Luke's home.

It was a very large apartment; besides the two lounges and the dining room, which she had already seen, and the nursery suite which was self-contained in that it held a bathroom, small kitchen as well as two bedrooms for Gianetta and Lucy, Anne found a study-library and three bedrooms, each with its own bathroom. Two of these rooms appeared to be guest rooms and the third was Luke's own. Anne stood on the threshold looking round; she did not have the feeling of interloping where she had no right to be, but at the same time, a bedroom was a personal place. It was a very masculine room decorated in quiet unassuming colors, the floor covered in green and white mosaic tiles, the furniture modern and good but functional rather than decorative. Despite the double bed with its green and brown bedspread, it was impossible to imagine Laura sharing this room with Luke. Laura would have slept in an ostentatiously feminine room, not this austere, cell-like place. This room showed a very different side of Luke. Anne would have expected antique furniture, perhaps the occasional photograph of Lucy or even Laura. But there was nothing of a personal nature anywhere. It was quiet and peaceful, overlooking the courtyard and thus away from the busy street, but had the air of a monk's cell. Sighing, wondering if she would ever truly understand this man whom she had learned to love in such an incredibly short time, Anne closed the door and returned to the nursery. As she crossed the hall, the telephone shrilled into the silence. While she wondered whether to answer it, Gina appeared, smiled at her and lifted the receiver. There followed a brief interchange in Italian and then Gina said to Anne, who had turned away, "It is Signor Patterson. He wishes to speak to you, signorina."

Delighted, Anne took the receiver. "Hello, Luke."

"Hello, my lovely. How are you this morning?"

"All the better for hearing from you," Anne smiled. "How did you know I'd be here?"

"I didn't. I just took a chance on it. I can't talk long. I'm up to my ears in work."

"Oh, dear. Problems?"

"Problems. Never mind, they'll sort themselves out. Did Gianetta ask you if you wanted to stay to lunch?"

"Yes, I intend to. Will you be here?"

"Unfortunately no. Don't bother to go back to your hotel this evening. I'll be home around six with luck."

"I'll need to go back to get changed," Anne said quickly. "I can't hang about in jeans all evening."

"I'm sure you look lovely. All right, but look, don't get all dressed up. I'm taking you out but it's a very casual place."

"I'll remember."

"See you tonight then. Love you."

Anne smiled happily. "Love you," she repeated, and warm delight flowed over her so that even after he had hung up the receiver on his end, she stood there listening to the clicking noises coming over the line. At last, catching sight of Gina's interested face, she colored faintly, but grinned and hung up, going hastily into the nursery.

It began by being one of the loveliest evenings

Anne had ever spent. Bearing in mind Luke's remarks about dressing casually, she wore the green pleated skirt that belonged to her suit, with a dark brown sweater, which Luke eyed approvingly when he came to meet her.

"You look more like a well-scrubbed English schoolgirl than ever," he smiled, kissing her gently. He wore a navy blue turtleneck sweater and slacks and a very expensive-looking, soft leather sports jacket; the lovely evocative smell of real leather came to Anne's nostrils as he momentarily held her against his shoulder.

"Where are we going?" Anne asked.

"Home first, to drop off the car. It's easier to walk in the center of Rome, or to get a cab. Besides, the place we're going isn't too far away."

They walked hand in hand down the Corso towards the Victor Emmanuel monument which stood out huge and white and ghostly in the gloom, its steps and statues illuminated by floodlights. Somewhere along here they moved off the well-lighted main street and in a while Luke steered Anne into a small restaurant. There were diners here already, eating at the small candle-lit tables. Luke led the way through the main restaurant and down some steps into a long, dimly lit cavernous place, illuminated by a candle at each table. From the ceiling hung Chianti bottles and cheeses and garlic sausages, and the most delicious smells pervaded the atmosphere. Anne gazed round her, delighted by this sight of real Rome. For the people who sat round them were mainly Italians.

A waiter appeared, greeting Luke with such a flood of Italian and so much laughter, that obviously Luke was well-known here. They were shown to a table by a huge, bewhiskered man, certainly the proprietor, who beamed delightedly at Anne, pulling out a chair for her with a flourish.

"I hope you like pizza," Luke said. "That's all they do down here."

"I do. I love it. Is that what all that means?" She indicated the menu which was in Italian.

"Yes. There are scores of varieties of pizza." He gave the order to the waiter. "I've ordered a fairly straightforward one for you. We can always come again to try something different. You should always drink beer with pizza," he added as the waiter placed two glasses and two litre bottles of Birra Peroni before them. Anne's eyes widened as they met Luke's over the candle flame. "I think it's just as well we walked," she smiled.

The food was brought by the proprietor himself. While Anne gazed in fascination at her plate—and the largest pizza she had ever seen, all cheesie and liberally covered with onion, tomato, olives and bacon—the Italian murmured something in a low voice to Luke who laughed and replied. Anne looked up quickly, sensing that the words had been about her.

"What did he say?" she asked.

"He said you have hair the color of flame," Luke

translated, adding to himself, "Among other things."

"What other things?"

"I'll spare your blushes, darling," he grinned. He was being so nice, almost boyish and certainly the most wonderful company, that Anne felt relaxed and content.

"Tell me what he said," she persisted.

Luke took a long drink of beer and looked solemnly at her over the rim of his glass. Then he shrugged. "He asked me whether all English girls were so eminently . . . bedworthy."

"Oh!"

"Well, you did ask."

"Yes," she admitted. "I did." Anne was very relieved that the place was so dimly lit for she had blushed fiery red. "Oh, you men!" she said crossly. "Don't you think of anything else?"

"Occasionally," he grinned. "You should take it as a compliment. Luigi wasn't being personal or familiar the way an Englishman or American would be if he said that. Italians have a regrettable tendency to speak very frankly about women."

"Obviously."

Luke finished his meal and pushed the plate away. "Darling, stop looking so . . . so affronted."

"I'm not!"

"You should see yourself." He put one hand on hers as it lay upon the table. "I'm glad you are, really. I wouldn't want you any other way. You're very different from Laura, aren't you?"

At the mention of her sister's name Anne's hand stiffened slightly in his hand and she had to force herself to relax.

"I don't know," she said. "Laura was more beautiful than I am."

"I didn't mean that. And it's not strictly true. I suppose superficially she was. She knew how to make the most of every asset she had—she used to drive me mad sometimes. The hours she would spend making herself up and having her hair done and her nails manicured."

"She was a model. She had to think of her appearance."

"I told you before that you don't have to defend her. I know all that. But she wasn't a model then. She was my wife and I didn't particularly want a wife who had to be gift wrapped."

It was a strange place to swap confidences and yet somehow the intimacy of the dark cellar prompted them both to say things which at some time or other would have to be said anyway. The soft whispered Italian voices around them were so uninterested in them that they might have been alone.

"You did love Laura though, didn't you?" Anne asked.

He lit cigarettes for them both and tipped the remaining beer into the glasses. In the glow of his cigarette lighter and the single candle flame, his face was somber and thoughtful. Anne saw the way the shadows played on the planes of his face, the way his eye lashes hooded his eyes. He said slowly, "I

. . . suppose I loved her. I was bowled over by her. She swept into my life like a wild, unmanageable hurricane and like any normal man I thought I could control her and mold her into my own image of what she should be. I couldn't, of course. I doubt that I made even a dent. She was a selfish . . . ." He halted, sharply cutting off the word "bitch," though Anne guessed it was coming. He said simply, "I thought that determination to possess another person, I suppose to own them body and soul, was what love was. It's all I've ever felt for any woman . . . until now."

"Now?" she prompted softly.

"I don't want to change you in any way, Anne. I don't want to force you into my way of life. I just want for you to have what's best for you." He took her hand again. "Look at me."

"Yes."

"I'm eleven years older than you—which isn't much I suppose. But in experience I guess I'm much older than you. I have a four-year-old daughter. . . ."

"Whom I love," Anne interrupted quickly, trying desperately to calm her thumping heart.

"I know you do. Anne, I can't think of anything I want more than for you to be my wife. But would it be right for you?"

"*I* can't think of anything that would be more right for me."

"Are you sure? It would mean living here in Rome. I do occasionally have to go to the States, but mostly

I live in Rome. It would mean leaving your family, your home."

Anne was trembling. "Don't keep making objections," she whispered. "You might talk yourself out of it. Oh, Luke, anywhere you are I want to be."

"It's crazy really," he murmured rubbing one hand over his hair in a slightly distracted way. "You hardly know me. We only met . . . God, four days ago. I must be crazy, asking you to marry me after only four days. You must be crazy even to contemplate it."

"Don't take it back, Luke," she said urgently. She sensed, womanlike, the correct way to handle the situation and her voice took on a slightly teasing note. "Don't you dare take it back. You can't go around asking people to marry you and then changing your mind."

"I haven't changed my mind. I want you . . . but you don't know me, Anne. I've got a lousy temper and I get moody and stiff-necked and . . . ."

"No one is nice and easy going all the time, Luke. I'm not—honestly. I get pig-headed and I sulk when I don't get my own way."

"I know how to deal with sulks," he said softly, and told her. Anne blushed rosily and smiled. By then she was in a very glow of happiness and delight. Luke paid the bill and they rose to venture out into the dark Rome night.

"I love Rome," Anne said as they walked up the stairs and into the top restaurant. "It would be lovely to live here."

"Wait till it's summer and ninety in the shade."

"I shan't mind. I shall laze on the balcony with a bottle of chilled wine and not do a thing."

"Lazy little cat." Briefly he put one arm across her shoulder and pressed her to him. As they came out of the restaurant a man was coming in and made to brush past them. For a moment all three of them halted in the doorway. It was dark but not too dark for Anne to see that Simon was looking very different from the way he had been the previous evening. He was dressed smartly in a lightweight suit and was cleanshaven and tidy. All three of them seemed to stiffen; Luke's hand, holding Anne's, tightened so much and so suddenly that she winced and felt as though the delicate bones would snap. Then Luke relaxed and said easily, "Hello, Simon. Where have you been lately?" His voice sounded merely pleasantly interested, but Anne's ears were attuned to his tones by now and she sensed the tension behind the casual words.

"Oh, I've been about." Simon looked at Anne and his smile broadened so that briefly again she saw the resemblance between him and Luke. "Anne, my dear, I didn't think I would see you again so soon. Two nights running. What a pleasure." He glanced quickly at Luke, then murmured, "Ciao, brother." This was all he said before moving into the restaurant but Anne caught a glimpse of something like a triumph on the weak, good-looking face. He had no need to say more; what few words he had uttered were enough to cause Anne's breath to draw in sharply and Luke's hand tightened again over hers.

"What the hell was all that about?" he demanded.

She realized then that had she mentioned earlier that she had met Simon, he would have thought nothing of it. It was the secretiveness of it that had angered him. As it was, the harshness of his voice, and the feeling that there was more here than met the eye, unnerved her so that instead of answering with the truth, she muttered, "I . . . I don't know," and then, "You're hurting my hand, Luke." She tried to pull away. The grasp on her hand loosened fractionally, though hardly enough to stop it hurting. He was walking fast and glancing up she saw that his face was set hard, his mouth tight and angry. Although this merely confirmed what she had suspected, that there was something very big and perhaps even frightening between him and Simon, she was upset and disturbed by this rapid, lightning change of mood.

"Slow down," she said. "I can't keep up with you."

"Are you going to tell me the truth?" he demanded, not even looking at her.

"Oh, don't be so dramatic!" she cried defensively, pulling away from him with one mighty effort. She rubbed her hand. "You don't have to resort to such caveman tactics, for heaven's sake!" She had stopped walking and now he turned to look at her.

"Well?"

"Well what? If you must know, I did see Simon last night. I went out with Tom and we met Simon in a horrible bar somewhere near the Pantheon. If you want the truth, I don't much care for your brother."

"Neither do I," he said dryly. "But I thought he was supposed to have a great fascination for women."

"I wouldn't know about that," she mumbled. She looked pointedly at the ground and walked up to and past him. He turned to walk beside her, hands deep in trouser pockets. The space between them was like a huge, unsurmountable wall, or a gaping chasm, made all the more bewildering to Anne because she did not know the cause of it. But suddenly she knew that Simon had arranged the "chance" meeting. He had known that Luke would react like this to her knowing him.

Luke raised one hand and called a taxicab, almost pushing Anne into the rear seat and following her in, saying "Hotel Tiber" in a curt voice. They sat in silence, the whole width of the seat between them as the car ran smoothly through the Roman streets. Anne stared numbly at Luke, but he seemed to be staring out of the window, deep in gloomy thoughts.

"You're right," she said abruptly. "You have got a lousy temper and you are moody and stiff-necked."

He took his eyes from the street and turned to look at her. After a moment he said, "Right. So you see what you'll have to put up with. I'm also possessive and bloody jealous." Next moment he was smiling and relief brought tears pricking at the back of Anne's eyes as his anger had not. Their hands touched and held and then with a sudden movement he came towards her, pulling her into his arms, his mouth pressing down on to hers. "I'm sorry," he whispered against her mouth. "I behaved stupidly and unreasonably. Darling, I can't explain, but please, please don't have anything to do with Simon. No." He stopped her interruption with his lips on hers. "Don't ask me why. Just believe me. He's poison."

"All right," she murmured. "I don't want to have anything to do with him anyway. Oh, Luke . . . ." He raised his head and said something to the driver who merely nodded his head phlegmatically.

"What did you say?" Anne asked.

"I told him to keep driving." He gave a little laugh that was not quite steady. "I think it must be over fifteen years since I had a necking session with a girl in the back of a cab."

Luke told the cab driver to wait while he went into the hotel with Anne. Alone in the lift, they kissed again and Anne clung to him. The last hour had been almost unbearably sweet; they had been driven through the night, she had no idea where, sometimes kissing, sometimes talking, silly love things that would have meant nothing to anyone else. Yet now she was frightened to leave him. It was a strange, unreasonable feeling that she could not explain. She wished the elevator had to go up fifty floors instead of just the one to the reception desk.

Luke looked round at the small bar-lounge. His eyes, accustomed to more luxurious surroundings, saw it as small and shabby. He would have liked to arrange for Anne to stay at a more expensive hotel;

he would willingly have footed the bill for her to go to the Rome Hilton, which lay in isolated splendor outside the city, but looking at her young, sweet face, all flushed and pink from his kisses, he knew better than to offer. He could imagine the dignified way she would refuse.

The young clerk, who had taken a fancy to Anne, smiled winningly at her and gave Luke an interested glance. He handed Anne her key.

"Signor Edwards telephoned, signorina. He said that he would call again in the morning."

"Oh, thank you."

"I thought Tom was staying here," Luke said.

"Yes, he was. He's gone south for a few days."

"Oh, Where?"

"I . . . don't know," Anne said. She wasn't a very good liar; he could tell from the way she refused to meet his eyes, while her cheeks reddened, that she was lying. Though why she should need to lie about such an unimportant thing he couldn't tell. He would have prodded the truth out of her but reckoned she had had enough for tonight. He had given her a rough enough time over Simon.

"Will you come and have lunch tomorrow at home?" he asked, before leaving her. "I should be able to take the afternoon off, provided there's no sudden crisis. Maybe we could go out somewhere, to Tivoli perhaps. It's well worth the drive."

"I'd love that."

"Come round any time you like." His mouth touched hers lightly. "Sleep well, carissima."

Although the lie she had told Luke troubled Anne, it did not stop her from sleeping. She felt secure and content in her love; Tom would return from Capri with no cause to believe Laura's death to be anymore than an accident, and with his suspicions totally unfounded. Soon the whole thing would be forgotten. There was no need to tell Luke about it, or the letter.

The letter still worried Anne a little—certainly more than she had let on to Tom. What was it all about? Twice now she had been witness to the fact that Luke did have a very quick and fairly violent temper so at least that part of the letter was true. Anne climbed into her cool narrow bed and closed her eyes. It would all come right in the end, she convinced herself, in much the same way that a child does. Luke had asked her to marry him and that, after all, had been the summit of her dreams since meeting him. With a contented little smile curving her lips, she curled up like a cat and was asleep.

Nine

Tom phoned the next morning when Anne was having breakfast. Eagerly she accepted the receiver from Guiseppe who was vastly intrigued by Anne and the fact that she apparently had two men chasing after her.

"Hello, Tom. Where are you?" she demanded without preamble.

"On Capri. I'm stopping in an hotel up in Anacapri. Hey, you were right about that road. It is pretty hair-raising."

"What have you been doing?"

"Oh, just poking around, asking a few questions here and there."

"And . . .?"

"No one seems very interested. It looks like you were right and it really was an accident. Still, I had one bit of luck. I got talking to a young fellow who used to work in the villa where Patterson and your sister were staying. The villa belongs to an American called Jack Marshall. Anyway, this chap told me your sister was in a helluva mood during the two days they were staying there. On the night before they left there was a full scale row which is why Luke decided to leave early. I gather Laura broke up the happy home throwing crockery about."

"Oh, dear," Anne said. Laura had done that at home more than once. She had always had a regrettable tendency to throw things when upset or thwarted.

"Apart from that, though, I couldn't find out anything," Tom continued. "My informant didn't know why the commotion and everyone seems to think the road really was so bad that if the brakes failed the car would have gone over the edge."

"So you're coming back?" Anne demanded eagerly. "You'll forget about it?"

"I suppose so," he agreed with regret. "I'm spending today doing a bit of sightseeing. I might as well while I'm here. I'll come back to Rome tomorrow. See you then."

The phone relieved Anne of a nagging feeling that Tom might be stirring things up too much. That morning she went to the Colisseum which she hadn't so far visited, but her visit was interrupted by a downpour of rain which forced her to take shelter. When the rain eased she decided to go straight to Luke's apartment. Thunder rumbled ominously in the distance now and she just made the apartment before the heavens opened. The rain hit the streets and pavements in a solid sheet that soon turned to hail. Anne shivered and pulled her jacket closer round her as she called the elevator

down and then sent it shooting up to the second
floor.

Gina was, as usual, all smiles. "Signor Patterson
is in the study," she said to Anne, indicating this
with a sweep of her hand. "He is on the telephone.
I will tell him you are here."

"There's no need. I'll go straight in," Anne told her.

Luke, wearing another very formal and smart
three-piece suit, was perched on the arm of a chair,
the telephone receiver to his ear. Anne heard him
shouting into it as she came in, but he wasn't angry,
except with the phone. He winked at her as she
entered, and put out one hand to her. She went
across to him and his arm tightened round her,
drawing her close to him. He kissed her slowly and
lingeringly and in the middle of the kiss she heard a
voice speaking in irate Italian through the receiver.
Luke drew back from her, replied in the same
language, and then, in English to Anne. "Won't be a
minute. Someone's trying to get through to me and
we keep getting cut off. Sit down. There's fresh
coffee in the pot. Hello . . . oh, for Christ's sake!
Blasted telephones."

"Don't blow a fuse," Anne smiled, pouring coffee.

"I won't. I . . . oh, hello, Jack, at last. What the hell's
been going on?" There was a long silence and then
Anne saw his smile turn to a frown. He glanced at
her once, looking at her almost as though she were a
stranger. "No," he said at length. "I didn't know
anything about it. Of course not. Thank you for
letting me know. . . . No, don't you do anything

about it. I'll see to it. Fine. Thanks, Jack. See you." He replaced the receiver very, very carefully, almost as though it were fragile and sat there, staring at the telephone as though he had never seen one before. Eventually he looked up at Anne. His face was expressionless. Not hard, nor angry, nor loving, just blank. But for a brief second Anne was sure pain had flickered through his eyes. She watched him light a cigarette and saw with amazement that his hand trembled. He seemed to notice this also, took a firm hold of himself and the trembling ceased. He drew hard on the cigarette as though his life depended on it.

"Where did you say Tom Edwards was?" he asked, not looking at her. He spoke softly, almost gently, but his words struck a chord of fear in Anne's brain.

"I didn't. He's down south somewhere."

"He's on Capri," Luke said. He looked at her now, narrow-eyed, through a haze of cigarette smoke. "As you no doubt knew. Didn't you?" When she made no answer, his voice hardened. "For God's sake, didn't you?"

"Yes."

"Yes. I won't ask why you lied since it's fairly obvious now. That was Jack Marshall on the phone. Ah, you recognize the name, do you? He has a villa on Capri. He thought he ought to call up and ask if I knew anything about some young English guy who's been making a few not very discreet enquiries about the accident that killed Laura. Jack isn't absolutely sure of the purpose of these enquiries but seems to think this guy is looking for evidence to prove it wasn't an accident." Anne raised her head and looked at him. She had gone pale and felt sick. This was like discovering that a nightmare had come true, and as in a bad dream she was totally unable to think coherently.

"Well?" Luke demanded. "Is that what he thinks?"

"I suppose so. I don't know what goes on in Tom's mind!"

"No. But I presume you know what goes on in your own mind. I suppose you must have told Tom Edwards how Laura died. Why, after all this time you should suddenly begin to think—whatever it is you do think . . . ."

"I don't think it," Anne whispered. "I never did, Luke. Truly I didn't."

"And I suppose you didn't know why Edwards went to Capri either. Come off it, darling, I wasn't born yesterday. My God, you really amaze me. Did you believe I wouldn't care that someone was going round suggesting things like that? I mean, you didn't think of warning me, or trying to stop him? For that matter, if you think I killed Laura, you sure are putting yourself at risk by being so often alone in my company. Who knows, I might start on you next."

"Luke, stop it!" Anne cried, jumping to her feet.

"You must let me explain. It isn't a bit like that. I never thought that about you. Not once!"

"Be quiet," he said icily. "Just be quiet. I don't want to hear your excuses. Sufficient that you saw fit to tell Tom Edwards about the accident. Oh, yes, my love, it was an accident. I'll admit there were numerous times when I would gladly have wrung Laura's neck, but I obviously have more forebearance than you would give me credit for."

"Luke, please let me . . . ."

"I don't want to hear." He sounded, not angry, but weary, and she knew how deeply he had been hurt. "If you start talking, I might just be talked round, and I have no intention of being talked round by you. That, if you remember, has already happened once. Well, it's not happening again." He stood up and walked to the door, opening it and calling, "Gina!" loudly. The Italian girl appeared.

"Signorina Markham is leaving. Show her out, please," he said quietly. He walked away, down the hall and into Lucy's nursery, closing the door very firmly behind him. Anne stared at his departing back and then at Gina. The girl's silent, interested presence stopped her from crying or running after Luke, or doing any of the things she wanted to do. Instead she walked past Gina and out of the front door.

"Goodbye, Gina," she whispered, turning once to look down the long hall to the room where Luke had gone.

"Arrivederci, signorina," Gina replied brightly. A lovers' tiff, she was thinking. Soon it would be made up; part of the joy of quarrelling was the making up.

It was still raining quite hard but Anne hardly noticed this. She turned left outside the building and walked down the Corso towards the Victor Emmanuel monument. Wasn't there some song called "Crying in the Rain?" It was supposed to stop people noticing you were crying. She would walk and walk and then perhaps she would forget that her own utter stupidity, that had prompted her to tell Tom things that did not concern him without even bothering to attempt to find out the truth herself, had caused her sweet dream, her lovely, lovely future to burn up into ashes. She didn't blame Luke for reacting as he had; she could only too well imagine how she would have felt if he had accused her of murder. But she hadn't really accused him, only by inference, yet she could not blame him for refusing to listen to her explanation. If he had seen the letter from Laura . . . she realized then that of course she should have shown him the letter. Perhaps she should have attacked—asked him what Laura had meant in the letter. It was just that she had been too stunned, too dismayed, to think straight.

But it was too late now. She couldn't go back, she couldn't beg. There didn't seem to be very much to do . . . except to go home to England. Disconsolately, not sure herself whether the wetness on her face was rain or tears or a mixture of both, she halted in mid-stride, turned right round and began to walk back in the direction of the hotel.

Luke stood in the window of Lucy's nursery, looking down at Anne's small, neat figure. She was almost out of sight when she changed direction and began to walk back up the street. For a moment he thought she was coming back, perhaps to try again to offer the explanation that he had refused to hear. But she walked on, head down against the rain, not even looking up. He was tempted to go and get her, or send Giovanni to pick her up, but he made no move. A drop of spring rain wouldn't do her much harm.

His initial reaction, on hearing what Tom Edwards was up to, had been disbelief. This was followed swiftly by such an interchange of emotions that he still felt numbed. Anger, disillusionment, bitter humiliation, pain, had all crowded in on him. Only after Anne was out of sight did he begin to wonder, what the hell were she and Tom Edwards up to anyway? Laura died over three years ago so why now start trying to make a big mystery of it? It didn't make sense. Perhaps Anne did have an explanation after all. But if she did he wasn't going to ask her for it. He was too emotionally involved with her and would never be able to judge rationally. He realized that he would want her explanation to be reasonable, that he would stretch things to make it so, to make it easier to take her back, to have her here, warm and soft and sweet in his arms. No, it was all too easy that way.

The logical solution came to him and he set about making arrangements. He was a man used to making swift decisions and when it came to it, he wasted no time. He put through a call to Capri and while the connection was being made quickly threw a change of clothes into an overnight bag and then rang through to Giovanni to have the car at the front door in half an hour. "The Porsche not the Cadillac, and I'll drive. Better get her filled up now." By then Jack Marshall was on the line from Capri. He asked Jack to find out something for him and left the line open twenty minutes while Jack got the required information. By then Giovanni was at the door with the dark blue Porsche. Then it remained only for him to request Gianetta to take care of Lucy for the next couple of days, to kiss Lucy goodbye and then to go to the car.

It was still raining and lightning flickered uneasily to the south of Rome, the direction he was heading, but he scarcely noticed this. He drove the Porsche just within the speed limit, heading out of the city and on to the autostrada, the Autostrada del Sole, the Road to the Sun. There was no real hurry. The hotel where Tom Edwards was staying had replied to Jack's queries, that Tom wasn't booking out till tomorrow, which probably meant he would catch the morning boat to Naples. That was, provided he didn't decide to go a different way to do some sightseeing, perhaps getting the Sorrento boat. Luke thought not. Edwards was following his journalistic nose, no matter how out of tune it happened to be, and wouldn't be turned off the scent even for such sights as Vesuvius and Pompeii. So, there was no hurry. But it took his mind off things to drive fast; the Cadillac was powerful but it was a prestige car; it made clients sit up and take notice. The Porsche was different; the Porsche reflected a usually submerged but fairly important part of his personality. The part that said, to hell with convention, with three-piece suits and business lunches, to such endless dullnesses as the submitting of estimates for contracts, checking on labor problems and building sites, and all the other necessary parts of his working life. The Porsche was part of the happier, relaxed and carefree side of his life, the side that Anne would have joined and enhanced. Damn and blast! Why should he think of that now? He jammed his foot down hard and then eased it as he saw a police car over on the left, heading towards Rome. There was no point getting a speeding ticket.

He stopped at a restaurant on the autostrada for a cup of strong black "expresso" coffee and stood by the car looking up at the foothills of the Apennines that ran all the way down this section of the autostrada, parallel to the road, reflecting gloomily that if he had obeyed his purely masculine instincts and made love to Anne, all this would have been unnecessary. Because if he had made love to her there would have been no going back on anything; he would have been entirely tied to her. He knew that without a doubt. It was ironic that for almost the first time in his life he had behaved altruistically and this was where it had got him.

"Oh, to hell with it," he muttered to himself, for the fiftieth time in the last couple of hours. He got into the car and drove on, hitting Naples just as the traffic was building up so that there was quite a long wait at the toll gate at the end of the motorway. By the time he had reached the thirty-block five-star hotel where he usually stopped when he was down this way, he was mentally exhausted. He dined alone and gloomy in the penthouse restaurant which offered magnificent views over Naples, its harbor and, when the day was clear, the whole of the bay, with Capri and Ischia clearly seen, and after drinking four or five double scotches in fairly rapid succession, went straight to bed and slept without a single dream to trouble his slumber.

Ten

If it were not for the fact that he was now experiencing it, Tom would never have believed how rough that tiny part of the Mediterranean known as the Bay of Naples could become. He left Capri gratefully, aware that somewhere along the line he had made a bit of a fool of himself, rushing about on a wild goose chase and that he would have to face Anne and admit this unsavory fact. They grey stormy sky, the driving rain which brought visibility down to a few hundred feet, so that he might almost have been on the Isle of Wight ferry instead of crossing from Capri to Naples, merely reflected his mood. By the time the boat had slid into the smooth but filthy waters of the port of Naples he was feeling thoroughly depressed and fed-up. There was only a scattering of people on the boat and he filed off with them, thinking dismally of the long bus journey back to Rome. He picked up his suitcase and set off across the docks to the road, his head sunk between his shoulders.

With the smooth efficiency of a well-planned operation, the dark blue Porsche slid to a purring halt beside him and Luke Patterson said, "Get in." Tom stared blankly at him and then, equally blankly, walked round to the left hand side of the car and got in. "There's a towel in the glove compartment," Luke said, and Tom took this out and rubbed it over his curling black hair.

"What the hell are you doing here?" he asked at last.

"Waiting for you, of course."

"How did you know I'd be on that boat?"

"I have . . . contacts." Luke took a packet of king size filter cigarettes from the top of the dashboard, lit one himself and tossed the packet to Tom who reflected that even foul American cigarettes were better than nothing. The rain slashed against the windscreen so that the wipers had all their work cut out to give any kind of visibility. Luke drove slowly, not talking, leaving Tom in a fever of curiosity and also faint annoyance. It was a relief to get a ride back to Rome but he wasn't too happy about the circumstances.

At last the rain eased a little and Luke was able to relax the intense concentration. He said, quite conversationally, "Well, I presume you discovered that I didn't kill my wife."

Tom gulped and stared at his profile, floundered uncertainly then muttered, "How do you know about that?"

147

"As I said, I have my contacts. Apparently your inquiries have been far from subtle. A friend of mine saw fit to inform me that you were asking questions of all and sundry."

"Yes . . . well, I'm a journalist. I couldn't let a story like that go past without doing a bit of digging. Anyway, there's no harm done."

"No harm done! God Almighty, there's a lot I could say about that! What the hell made you both think it in the first place, that's what I'd like to know."

"Both of us?" Tom repeated. "Anne didn't think it. At least, once she'd met you she didn't. And it was me put the idea into her head in the first place. Here, have you talked to her about this?"

"You might say the subject came up," Luke said with dry grimness.

"Well, don't go blaming her. She tried to stop me going to Capri. I think she wished she'd never shown me the letter in the first place. And you can't blame either of us jumping to conclusions after reading it. You've got to admit it's queer, and I'd still like to know. . . ."

"Wait a minute," Luke interrupted. "What letter?"

"The letter from Laura."

"I don't know anything about any letter."

"Didn't Anne explain about it then, when you talked about this?"

Luke took a very deep breath then said in a low voice, "I didn't exactly give her a chance to explain anything. I suppose you'd better tell me about it."

Tom did, swiftly and succinctly, in his best journalistic style, beginning with his meeting with Anne on the plane. Luke listened in silence, not once taking his eyes off the long wet ribbon of the autostrada that stretched before him. When Tom had finished there was a brief silence than Luke said, heavily, "Yes, it makes sense. I can't say I blame you for wondering. Now listen, this is not for publication, mind, and by Christ you'd better remember that . . . I'll tell you what I think that letter meant. . . ."

They had lunch in Formia, taking their time to get back to Rome. By then there was a fairly relaxed atmosphere between the two men and Tom had decided that Luke Patterson wasn't such a bad bloke after all.

"You going to marry Anne?" Tom asked, digging into his Cannelloni with relish.

"If she'll have me. Which, after the hard time I gave her, I doubt."

"Oh, she'll come round. Women always do."

"There speaks the voice of experience. Did you have any aims in that direction?"

"Me? Not likely. Not my type at all. I wouldn't have thought she was yours either. I mean, Anne's a nice girl, quite good-looking. But not exactly in the same class as . . . well, as Elise Carr for example."

"Thank God! I wouldn't have contemplated marrying her if she were. Laura was that type and one marriage of that kind is enough for any man. You want to keep away from Elise and her sort. She'd eat you for breakfast."

"That's word for word what I told Anne you'd do to her," Tom said dryly, and Luke grinned.

"I'll try to control my carnivorous instincts."

When they reached Rome, Luke drove straight to the Hotel Tiber. "Better get my apologies over with," he told Tom.

"You'll probably have to crawl," Tom said with malicious pleasure. "There's nothing a woman likes better than to see a bloke cringing in abject misery before her."

"Shut up," Luke said getting out of the car. "And stay here. If I have to crawl I don't want you witnessing it."

Nevertheless, masculine-like, he was feeling fairly sure of himself as he went up to the reception desk and inquired after Anne. There wouldn't be much crawling or apologizing to do. It came as more than a shock when the clerk said, "I am sorry, signore, but Signorina Markham is not here."

Luke glanced at his watch. It was six-thirty. "You mean she hasn't come in for dinner yet?"

"She never came back for lunch, signore. She went out this morning at about ten-thirty. She said to me as she went out that she would be back for lunch but she did not return. Neither did she telephone to let us know. And now, signore, it wants but half an hour to dinner time and see, the key to Signorina Markham's room is still there." He indicated the key board.

Luke frowned, puzzled, a little worried. "You have no idea where she went this morning?"

"No, signore."

Tom was still in the car. Confronted with the problem, he said at once, "I reckon she'll be at your place. It's obvious she'd have gone back this morning. Perhaps she intended showing you the letter from Laura. Finding you not there she'll have stayed the day with your daughter."

After the way he had virtually thrown her out yesterday, Luke doubted that Anne would do any such thing, but he couldn't think where else she could be. "Sure, that might be it," he agreed. "Let's go."

But they were greeted at the front door of the apartment, which was flung open almost before Luke could get his key in the lock, by an excitable and tearful Gianetta. In the background, looking equally distressed, were Giovanni, Luke's chauffeur, Gina the maid and Signora Verdi. Gianetta let out such a flood of volatile, rapid Italian that Tom had no hope of understanding it. But it only took common sense to know that what she said merely increased Luke's concern. Not only did his expression become very grave but he also went quite pale. His voice was tense as he questioned Gianetta.

"What is it?" Tom asked fearfully.

"I left Gianetta in charge of Lucy," Luke explained. "She says Simon came here this morning and gave her the day off. Simon told her he'd-seen me and told me he would take Lucy off for the day. She had no reason to doubt him."

"Simon," Tom repeated thoughtfully.

"If he really only intended taking her out, he would have brought her back by now."

"An accident?" Tom queried.

Luke shook his head. "Somehow I don't think so. Why the hell should Simon take it into his head to go off with Lucy like that?"

Gianetta uttered another burst of Italian which started them all off this time, all the staff anxious to get in their own words. In between the shouting, Gina handed something to Luke. It was a small white handkerchief, lace edged with the initial A in the corner.

"That's Anne's," Tom said.

"I know. Gina found it here. She says she cleared up this morning and it definitely wasn't here then. That means Anne has been here . . . and the chances are that both she and Lucy are with Simon. Look, if Anne left this, maybe on purpose, she may have left something else. We can't just go charging round searching without direction."

"The police?" Tom suggested, but Luke shook his head violently.

"Not yet! You know what I told you about Simon earlier. There's no knowing what he'll do if he thinks he's being hounded. No, we must search the apart-

ment thoroughly." He told the staff and they obediently scattered. It was Giovanni who found the
letters FRA scrawled in Anne's lipstick beside the
washbasin in the nursery bathroom. He called Luke
and everyone gathered to look in puzzlement at the
small pink letters.

"FRA? What the hell does that mean?" Tom
asked.

"I don't know. But it must mean something."

"Do those letters stand for something—or someone's initials?"

"Not that I know of."

"Then a place beginning with. . . ."

"Frascati!" Luke yelled. "My God, I'm a bloody fool.
Of course, Frascati." He was already striding towards the door. "Come on, Tom. And, Gianetta, will
you stay here? In case I need to call you?"

"Si, signore. Signore, I am sorry." Even in his
hurry Luke paused a second to soothe the tearful
girl.

"It's not your fault, Gianetta. I should have
warned you about Simon. I just never thought. . . ."
He smiled briefly but his eyes were bleak. "If anything happens to them it'll be my fault."

Luke set the Porsche on the road to Frascati. Tom
glanced fearfully at his hard, still profile, the eyes
staring unblinkingly at the road. As soon as they
were out of Rome, Luke jammed his foot down and
the powerful car let out a roar and leapt forward.
Tom, who was not normally worried about speed,
felt a little tug of fear. He wouldn't like to be in

Simon's shoes if he had laid one hand on Lucy or Anne. There was a deadly, implacable look about Luke Patterson that totally belied his normally charming, benign character.

"What's in Frascati?" he asked.

"I have a villa there. It hasn't been used in God knows how long. I'd never have thought of looking there. When Laura died I had it closed up. She used it a lot . . . to entertain her lovers."

"Including Simon?"

"Especially Simon."

"What do you think he intends to do?"

"How the hell should I know?" Luke snarled savagely. "But if he hurts them. . . ."

"He won't though, will he? If what you said earlier is true. . . ."

"If you mean because he must love Lucy, you couldn't be more wrong. Simon doesn't know how to love anyone. To him Lucy has always been a tool to get at me. He knew there was little I could do about it. There's always been the thought that one day he might tell her everything. Even now, young as she is and not completely understanding, the truth could damage her. That's why I've put up with him all these years. It was a sort of blackmail, I suppose, far worse than the usual kind. Because of Lucy he had a hold on me and how he enjoyed that."

"But what's Anne doing with him?"

Luke shook his head, still not taking his eyes from the long winding road. They were high up now, in the hills above Rome, and the road was narrower and beginning to twist, but Luke did not once slacken speed. "I don't know why she went with him. Maybe he forced her. Maybe she went of her own accord."

"She wouldn't do that," Tom said confidently. "Unless she went because of Lucy. She hates Simon. She wouldn't go anywhere with him willingly."

When morning had dawned Anne had known she would have to try just once more to explain to Luke about Laura's letter. What was the point of stiff-necked pride when her happiness and Luke's also was at stake? She lay in bed listening to the rain that still splashed against her window, while her body ached with unhappiness at the thought of Luke's scathing words. Damn it, she would make him listen! She would see him, phone him, write to him, keep on and on till he had to listen out of sheer self-defense. She would not lose this man whom she loved so very much, because of a misunderstanding.

So she went to his apartment mid-morning, wearing a lightweight raincoat. She rang the bell determined to force her way in if necessary.

The door was opened, surprisingly, by Simon. He held the door ajar about eight inches and peered at her through the gap. He was looking wary but a measure of relief crossed his face when he saw her. Remembering the last time she had seen him, outside the restaurant Luke had taken her to, Anne recoiled slightly.

"Oh, it's you," he muttered.

"It is. I want to see Luke."

"He's not here."

She was not prepared for this and was momentarily stumped. "I suppose he's at work. I'll come in and wait till he comes home."

"He won't be home till late and he's not at work. He left last night. He asked Gianetta to look after Lucy and then drove off somewhere. All very mysterious."

"Oh . . . well . . . can I see Gianetta?"

"She's not here."

"Gina then."

"She's got the day off."

He spoke quietly, a trifle breathlessly and Anne was conscious of a great tension in him. She frowned, puzzled, aware that something was vastly wrong but unable to put her finger on what it was. Simon was still peering at her through a narrow gap in the door. She tried to look beyond him but couldn't.

"Is Lucy here?" she asked and he nodded.

"Who's looking after her?"

"I am."

"Well, could I see her?"

He began to look mulish, a little angry, his mouth hardening into a tight, white line, so that she expected him to deny her this request as he had the others. Instead he nodded and stood back, saying, "Come in then." She was hardly inside the door before he slammed it shut behind her. She looked, startled, at him, then glanced round the hall, but everything seemed perfectly normal, everything except the small suitcase packed up and standing near the hall table, obviously waiting to be taken off somewhere. On top of the case was one of Lucy's dolls. Anne looked at the case, then at Simon. The tight look was more pronounced now.

"What is all this?" Anne demanded.

"What does it look like?" he snarled.

Suddenly Anne shuddered. She didn't know why a black feeling of sheer terror shook her, but as it did she knew that Simon sensed it. She remembered the look of almost impotent fury she had once seen on Luke's face when Simon went to see Lucy; at last she realized that there had been fear mixed with that fury.

"Where is Lucy?" she demanded in a hoarse voice. "Where is she?"

"Don't be so intense, baby," he drawled, smiling and quite abruptly looking fairly normal. "Do you think I'd harm her?"

So saying, he pushed open the nursery door and Anne saw Lucy on her rocking horse. Sick with relief she went over to the child and lifted her off the horse, hugging her fiercely. Lucy accepted this treatment with admirable aplomb, finally pulling away and saying, "Are you coming with us, Anne?"

"Coming where, Lucy?"

"With Uncle Simon. I was allowed to pack my own suitcase. We're going a long way, aren't we, Uncle Simon?"

"That's right, Lucy, on a long journey," Simon agreed, pleasantly, not taking his eyes off Anne's face.

"What are you talking about?" Anne whispered, turning so that Lucy could not hear her. "Where are you going? And where's Luke? For God's sake, Simon, what are you . . . ?"

"Shut up!" he hissed. He grabbed her roughly and hauled her out of the room shutting the door firmly. With a slender but surprisingly strong arm, he flung her against the wall and approached to stand before her. There was glittering laughter on his face, laughter that held a trace of madness and turned Anne's blood to ice. "I'm going, Anne darling, and taking Lucy with me. That's what it's all about. I don't know where Luke is. He told Gianetta he'd be home some time after mid-day, which still gives me a couple of hours. Frankly I don't care if I never see the bastard again. I don't like my big brother, Annie, my sweet. He's a smug, self-righteous bastard who seems to think he has the right to control my life. Well, just now I'm doing the controlling. I'm taking Lucy with me and you, my love, since you're here, can come with us."

"I won't! And you can't make me!"

"I could try, and that would frighten Lucy. At the moment she's quite happy. That's the reason you'll come, to make sure she stays happy and looked after. Yes, you might prove useful. Besides, I'd be a fool to turn down your company. You're quite something, Annie, and I really go for that sweet, innocent look. Why, you and I might suit very well." As he spoke he had moved closer and now he put one hand against Anne's neck. Her eyes widened as she realized his intention. She moved swiftly, slipping away from him as he bent his head towards her.

"You're mad!" she cried. "You must be. What's the *point* of all this, for heaven's sake? It doesn't make sense. Are you trying to kidnap Lucy? Is it money you want from Luke?"

He wasn't put out by her abrupt refusal of him. Why should he be. There would be time enough in the future to persuade her . . . or force her, to change her mind. He laughed now. "No, I don't want his money. I want to see him crawl. He can crawl for Lucy and, by God, he can crawl for you too. You might not be quite so sweet and untarnished as when he lost you, but still, no matter. No, Anne. I'm not kidnapping Lucy. A man doesn't need to kidnap his own daughter."

Now Anne was sure he was mad. She found she could no longer think lucidly. All she knew was that Lucy must not be alarmed; she must somehow keep calm and level headed, convincing the child that everything was normal.

"You don't believe me, do you?" Simon smiled. "You don't believe Lucy is my daughter. I suppose you think no woman could look at me after she'd had the great Luke." His voice sneered cruelly. "You didn't know your sister very well, obviously. She was no more than a tramp. Oh, a very high class tramp.

No rubbish for Laura. But she wasn't the sort to stick to one guy very long. We had a great time together—sometimes when I was in Rome and Luke was away on business. Once she flew out to me in New York. Oh, a rare one was Laura, I can tell you."

As he spoke it seemed to Anne that she might actually be sick, physically sick there and then, and she covered her mouth as though this could prevent her from retching. Yet through it all, her main thought was that suddenly she knew what Simon said was the truth.

"How could you know about Lucy?" she asked. "You and Luke are so alike that Lucy looking like you means nothing."

"Oh, I know she's mine all right. You see, Luke's a proud sort of guy, not one to have anything to do with a wife who was carrying on with his own brother. He and Laura even had separate bedrooms. There hadn't been anything between them for almost a year. They just seemed like a real loving couple but believe me, that was a mighty false impression."

"But. . . ." Anne began to object, however, he stopped her, glancing at his watch.

"Enough. I don't mind telling you all you want to know—once we're on the way. But he might be arriving back soon and I've no intention of letting this opportunity slip through my fingers."

Any hope Anne had of delaying him until Luke appeared slipped away. "Where are you taking us?"

she asked dully, without much hope of being told.

But Simon was feeling good, sure of himself, in control of the situation, full of self confidence. "To Frascati first. Luke's got a villa up there, but he never uses it. It's locked up and deserted. We'll stay there for a couple of days. When Luke finds Lucy has gone he'll soon have the cops looking for her. So we'll wait till the hunt dies down. They'll never think of looking so close to Rome."

"And then?"

"And then we'll head north, over the border into Austria. I've got one or two friends there who owe me. They'll hide us for a while. Now, no more questions. Get Lucy ready and don't try drawing attention to us when we get outside. Don't forget, I don't love Lucy even if she is my daughter. It wouldn't bother me if she got frightened, or even hurt. Get me?"

"Yes. I'll fetch her."

Lucy allowed Anne to help her into her bright red and yellow raincoat with matching boots and rain hat, and chattered excitedly as she did so. Anne tried hard to smile and behave normally but knowing what she did, this was not easy. She looked closely at Lucy, glad that she still loved the little girl even though she now knew she wasn't Luke's own daughter. After all, Luke himself knew—obviously he did if the facts Simon had told her were true. Yet he loved Lucy.

Simon was waiting for them by the open nursery

door. As she came out with Lucy, Anne said, "Can you wait a minute? Lucy probably ought to go to the bathroom."

Simon stared uncomprehendingly at her, then understanding dawned. "All right," he agreed begrudgingly. "But don't take all day."

In the nursery bathroom Anne worked quickly. While Lucy was telling her loudly and emphatically that she did *not* want to use the toilet, Anne pulled the lipstick from her make-up bag and scrawled FRASCATI on the tiles by the bath. Lucy watched interestedly.

"What's that for?"

"Shush!" Anne whispered. "It's a sort of game. You mustn't say anything."

Lucy nodded, obediently clamping her mouth shut. The pink letters stood out strongly and surely someone would see them . . . Simon included. Suppose he looked in? He wasn't a fool. Hastily Anne began to write again, smaller this time, low down behind the washbasin. She had only written the first three letters when Simon opened the door.

"Come on, for Christ's sake!" he growled. Anne had sprung away from the washbasin as soon as she heard the door, but she stood in the middle of the room guiltily holding her lipstick. Simon's eyes went straight to the large red letters by the bath. For a moment his expression took on an ugly look but this cleared almost at once. He rather admired her for trying.

"Rub it off!" he said softly. He stood watching as

she wiped off the marks with toilet paper. Then she took Lucy's hand and walked past Simon. He grabbed her arm as she went by and she looked up at him fearfully. His fingers bit cruelly into her arm.

"Don't try anything else, beautiful. One try is fair enough but next time I might just make you regret it."

They went down to the street in the lift and then along the road to where Simon's Maserati was parked. Anne took Lucy on her lap and fixed the safety belt round both of them. She had almost given up hope. How would Luke see those three small letters down by the washbasin?

At the thought of Luke she could have cried. Where was he? How would he feel when he returned home and found Lucy gone? The silly misunderstanding between herself and Luke seemed strangely unimportant now. What did it matter if Luke thought she believed he had murdered Laura, when here were she and Lucy in the clutches of a potentially dangerous man? That he was dangerous, Anne did not doubt. She looked surreptitiously at Simon. He was relaxed in the driver's seat, his hands resting lightly on the wheel and every now and then he smiled to himself and once he even laughed out loud. Anne felt a renewal of fear. How did he intend to make Luke "crawl," as he had so horribly put it?

They were out of Rome now, climbing up into the Alban Hills. This was a one time volcanic area, topped by Monte Cavo which was over nine hundred meters high. Anne remembered reading about this area before leaving home, when she had made the effort to learn something of Rome and its environs. There were several craters of various sizes which had, over the years, filled with water and were now beautiful lakes that provided homes for a variety of water birds. The road was bordered by vineyards, lush and green, and the paler silver-green of olives. The rain continued in a miserable and steady drizzle and no one was working in the fields. When Anne twisted round to look back towards Rome she could see nothing but mist. It was as though they were heading right up into the clouds, for the hills ahead of them were also shrouded. The powerful car drove on in a world of its own, a world peopled by only the three who sat in it.

"It's no good looking for help," Simon said pleasantly. "There's no knight in armor coming to rescue you. Your precious Luke is miles away and he'll never think of coming here. He hates the place like poison, ever since the day he came up here and found Laura and me together." His hands tightened convulsively on the wheel. "That's just one more score to be settled, Mr. Luke Patterson. By God, they all add up to a very pretty total. Do you know what the bastard did? He stormed in on us like a Victorian husband. . . ." His voice had risen to a shout and Anne clamped her hands over Lucy's ears, thankful that the child was now asleep and praying she would not waken. "He dragged me outside and he hit me—that's what! With Laura there watching. He hit me and hit me, and she, the bitch, stood there half-naked and enjoyed it. She liked the idea of men fighting over her. But she got her just deserts. He dragged her off home and I know for a certainty he never went near her again."

Hoping to calm him, Anne asked quietly, "Was this before Lucy was born?"

"That's right. Naturally Laura and I got together again. I wasn't going to let that sod dictate to me. Anyway, that's how he knew Lucy wasn't his."

"Yet he accepted Lucy as his own."

"Yeah. He's soft. You wouldn't catch me taking on someone else's kid."

"No. But then, you and Luke aren't really alike, are you?" Anne flashed.

"Too bloody right we're not! I never did understand what makes him tick. He's hard as nails in business—and with me—yet he took Laura back and brought up our kid. Can you imagine that? I'm damned if I would. No one double-crosses me and gets away with it."

Lucy—thank goodness!—was still sleeping soundly in Anne's arms, her thumb tight in her mouth. Anne guessed from the height they had climbed that they must be near Frascati now, though with the driving rain that lashed the windscreen it was impossible to see much. Simon seemed to know the road well.

Suddenly Anne knew that if anyone could tell her about Laura's letter, Simon could. "Did Tom tell you about the letter I had from Laura?" she asked in a low voice. "The letter saying she had something to tell Luke, and that she was frightened of what his reaction would be?"

Simon laughed. "Yeah, he told me. The poor sucker. He got this crazy idea that Luke killed Laura. Can you imagine that? Luke's too bloody civilized to do anything like that."

"You led us to believe Luke might have done it!" Anne cried.

"Sure. Why not? It was a laugh to make someone believe that about Luke. No one ever thinks anything bad about Luke," he sneered. "I wish I'd thought of that one before. It would have been easy enough to make it look like murder."

"What do you mean?" Anne whispered, but Simon seemed to realize he had said too much and refused to enlighten her. He drove in silence now and at length pulled the car up before a low-roofed white building with a covered veranda along the front and a porch supported by six slender pillars. The drive was bordered by rose bushes, azaleas, rhododendrons and the occasional oleander, all overgrown and wind and rainswept. Anne carried the now awake Lucy and put her down on the porch while Simon opened the door.

"I always kept the key," he said. "You never know when a key might come in useful."

"Where are we?" Lucy asked, slipping her hand into Anne's. "Where's my daddy?"

Anne strove to appear cheerful for the child's sake, as she told her that the house belonged to her

Daddy. Lucy seemed happy enough at the moment. When they entered the dark, musty house that was cobwebby and dusty, she explored with interest, not a bit put out by the murky atmosphere.

"This'll do nicely for a couple of days," Simon nodded. "No one will look here."

"You can't keep us here," Anne hissed at him. "You know you can't. They'll look for us."

"Sure they will. But they won't look here."

"Listen, Simon, let Lucy and me go. I promise we won't tell anyone where you are."

He laughed. "What would be the point of that? Do you think Luke gives a damn where I am, so long as I'm not anywhere near him or his precious Lucy? The whole point of this operation is that you and Lucy are both here, in my power. No, my sweet, we'll stay here a few days, then head for Austria. When Luke's half out of his mind with worry, then I might just turn the screw a little—send him a lock of Lucy's hair or something of that sort." His eyes blazed fanatically as he envisaged revenge for slights real or imagined, so that Anne felt ill with fear for the child and herself. She glanced fearfully towards Lucy who was intent on drawing pictures on the grimy windows with one equally grimy finger and completely ignoring the adults.

"I'm sure Luke would pay you anything you want if. . . ."

"I told you before, I don't want money! He's got so much of that it wouldn't hurt him to part with it. I just want him to suffer. I took his wife and that was sweet revenge but it didn't hurt him, only his pride. He didn't care that much about her. Christ, but I wish I'd thought of framing Luke for Laura's murder! I was a fool to let that one pass!"

"What do you mean?" Anne cried.

"What do you think? Didn't you know, Anne? I was on Capri that day too. I was staying with Jack Marshall. There was an almighty row between Luke and Laura that morning. She was in a hell of a state because she was pregnant again and hadn't got the nerve to tell Luke. That's what it was all about, sweet Anne. She'd already had Lucy, who was mine, and now she was pregnant again. God knows who the kid belonged to. It wasn't mine and it certainly wasn't Luke's. But she knew she'd have to tell him. She thought he would probably divorce her and she couldn't stand the thought of that. Whatever she felt for Luke, he was rich enough to keep her in luxury. She wanted me to help her and when I refused she threatened to tell Luke that the baby was mine. I couldn't have that, could I? At that time I'd just got back into Luke's good books. Then I heard they were driving down to the boat and I thought of a fine opportunity to kill two birds with one stone, quite literally at that. I could get rid of Laura who was getting to be a blasted nuisance, and Luke as well. After all, our father is a very rich man and he only has two sons."

It seemed to Anne that she was listening to all this through a long, dark tunnel. It all was so clear and so obvious now that she knew. What diabolical rancor had swelled in Simon all these years! What terrible emotions had become churned and twisted in him, and finally become unleashed by Tom's probings! She sat down abruptly as her knees gave out, and a gentle cloud of dust rose from the cushioned seat.

"You killed Laura," she whispered.

"It should have been both of them. He had the luck of the devil to escape completely unhurt, without even a scratch. The car was a write-off so no one ever knew I'd cut through the hydraulic system." He smiled again, a sweet and gentle smile that struck Anne cold right through. "You know what they say, honey, the first murder is the worst. After that it gets easier. I have nothing to lose now. It wouldn't bother me to kill you, to put my hands round that sweet neck of yours and squeeze and squeeze . . . it would be a shame since we could have such fun together, but don't think it would worry me."

Unbidden, Anne's hands went to her neck, almost as though she could feel Simon's long, slender fingers encircling it. At that moment Lucy left her picture drawing and came running down the long room to them. She smiled winningly at Simon and said, "Can we go? I don't like it here much. It smells funny."

Anne reached out and grabbed her, pulling her away from Simon and holding her tightly, a movement that Simon seemed to find enormously funny. "Be patient, darling. We won't be long."

"I want my Daddy," Lucy told her. "He promised to bring me back a present. Where is he?"

"He'll come as soon as he can, love," Anne said, smiling with an effort. "We must just be patient."

"That's right," Simon agreed. "Be patient."

For the rest of the afternoon events gradually took on a nightmare aspect to Anne. Trying to keep Lucy from getting upset, faced with the prospect of two or three days in this place with no food and no chance of rescue, she sometimes felt like crying with helplessness. No one would find her message, or, finding it, understand it. Then she thought, perhaps she should try to escape. Surely Simon would have to sleep. He couldn't watch them all the time. She knew she would have no compunction about hitting Simon over the head in order that she and Lucy could get away, and there were plenty of objects that might make suitable weapons. The room where they sat was littered with vases, heavy books, and an assortment of ornaments, any of which would easily knock a man out. Her attitude towards Simon took on a ruthlessness towards evening when it was no longer possible to comfort Lucy. She was a bright, intelligent child who soon guessed that something was vastly wrong. At first, getting no real answer from Anne, she ran to Simon.

"Uncle Simon, please can we go home?" she cried, and he, nerves strung tight as problems that he had not foreseen, these chiefly being lack of food and electricity, came to mind, turned on her, pushing her away. "You aren't going anywhere, brat! So keep out of my way!" he yelled. Simultaneously, Lucy broke into screams of fear and Anne rushed over to her, lifting her in her arms.

"You brute!" she cried. "How could you?"

"Shut up," he snarled. "And keep her out of my way. Sit down over there where I can keep an eye on you."

"You can't watch us all the time," Anne said. She broke off her words sharply, realizing she should never have reminded him of this, but it was too late. She had put him on his guard. He looked narrow eyed at her and then, before she could move, grabbed her arm. "Come on."

"Where?"

"Never mind. Just come."

Eleven

Often afterwards Anne wondered why she had followed Simon's instructions so obediently. He had no gun with which to threaten her. But Lucy's presence prevented her attempting to escape while Simon was still fully alert. It would be so easy for him to hurt Lucy. As it was, she was already a frightened, tearful girl.

Simon pushed them on ahead of him out of the front door and across the muddy forecourt, round the side of the house to where there was a small brick built garden shed. There was a strong padlock on the door but he remembered where the key was. He knew this shed of old. It was here that he had first become Laura's lover. They had often met here, sometimes enjoying the added spice of knowing that Luke was actually in the house. He found the key on a ledge above the door and soon had Anne and Lucy inside.

"Sit down there." He indicated a pile of sacks. Anne sat on them and watched as he found a coil of thin wire. Anne knew then that she would have to do something, for once tied up and locked in they would be completely helpless. Not stopping to think, not daring to think, she flung herself at Simon's legs, at the same time yelling, "Run, Lucy, run!" Next moment the world exploded in stars that whirled about her, as Simon's fist caught her on the side of her jaw. . . .

When Anne came to she was lying on her side, her face pressed into the foul smelling sacks. She tried to move and pain exploded in her face and in her wrists and ankles. It took only a second for her to realize that her arms and legs were bound by the wire Simon had found, wire that bit cruelly into her soft flesh. She bit back the cry of pain as she struggled to sit up. Her arms were tied in front of her and her fingers were free but though she tried she could not even move the wire round her ankles and when she did try it only caused the wire to dig more tightly into her. The effort exhausted her and she flopped back on to the sacks, determined not to give way to the tears that were pricking at her eyelids.

Then all thoughts of her own pain and discomfort vanished as she remembered Lucy. The little hut was in semi-darkness; what little daylight there was left outside found short shift through the narrow dirty window, but she could tell that she was alone and her panic-stricken shout of the child's name brought no answering cry. She struggled to sit up again, fighting back the nausea as the wire tightened over wrists and ankles, calling out Lucy's name again and again. In between these cries, feverish muttered prayers tumbled one after the other from her lips. It was no good. She could not even get to her feet. Simon had crossed her legs before tying them and it was impossible for her to stand up. She fell back again, crying now without attempting to stem the tears. It was all her fault. Surely she could have thought of something before they arrived at the villa! She could have got away somehow. Lucy must have obeyed her order to run and Simon would have tied her, Anne, up and then gone out to search for her. Simon who had admitted that he cared nothing for the child. Simon who had said it would not be so hard to murder a second time. What would he do to her?

"Oh, God, please help," she whispered into the pile of sacks. "Don't let him hurt her, God, please, please. . . ."

The silence in the hut was broken by a sudden bang so close that Anne yelped with fright. There was the sound of splintering wood and next moment the door opened, its padlock hanging off where the axe had cut through the rotten wood. With a sob of fear, sure that Simon had come back seeking revenge for her act of rebellion, she shrank back into the sacks, biting her lip to stop herself crying out, only partially hearing Luke say, "Oh, my God," as he saw her. Then with a leap that took him clear across the hut, he was beside her, gathering her up in his strong arms, holding her and kissing her as though he knew how close he had been to losing her.

Even through the ecstasy of being in his arms, of having her fears vanquished so abruptly, two thoughts were in Anne's mind. She cried out, "Oh, Luke . . . Lucy. . . ." And then, because she could not stand it any longer, because she thought she might pass out, "My hands. . . ."

When he had grasped her, her hands had been pulled cruelly against the wire that bound them. Luke moved back and looked, swearing harshly as he saw how the delicate skin of her wrists was chaffed and in some places torn and bleeding. He left her a moment, searching feverishly until he found a pair of wire clippers, kneeling down beside her and setting to work with grim determination.

"I'm bound to hurt you more. I'll try not to."

"It can't hurt anymore. Luke, Lucy ran away. I don't know where she is."

"She's all right. She's with Tom. Try to keep still, darling. Just three more to go. God, if I'd known he had done this to you I would have killed him." The final wire parted with a little twang! and Anne let out an involuntary cry as the feeling began to return to her numbed hands. Luke started on the wire round her ankles while she gingerly moved her fingers, trying not to make a sound. Luke finished his task and looked up at her. She noticed how dirty he was, covered in mud and soaked to the skin. Beneath the mud, his face, as he turned it towards her, was numb with adoration.

"I thought I had lost you both," he whispered hoarsely. "Oh, Christ, Anne, I love you so much."

She managed to smile through her pain and tears. With great gentleness he reached out for her, lifting her in his arms and holding her against him, stroking her hair and murmuring soothing things into her ear. Words tumbled from her, hasty and not very coherent, as she told him what Simon's intentions had been. She made no mention of Laura's "accident" and even now knew that she never would. That would be too much for Luke to bear. Even as she mentioned the lesser of Simon's iniquities she felt Luke stiffen, and then his hands continued their rhythmic stroking of her hair and back. He rocked her gently in his arms as though she were a child, so that suddenly all she wanted to do was sleep, just to close her eyes and give herself up to his strong, beloved presence. But first there was something else that had to be said, now while they were quiet and alone. She pulled back and looked up at him.

"Luke . . . Simon said that . . . that Lucy . . ." she halted, uncertain and miserable, seeing the closed up, hurt look that moved across his face. She shook her head. "I'm sorry. I shouldn't have . . . it doesn't matter."

"What did he say about Lucy?" he asked quietly.

"He said she was his daughter."

A long drawn out sigh shuddered through Luke's body so that for a moment Anne felt that she was the stronger. Ignoring her own aches and pains she flung her arms about him, pulling his head down upon her shoulder. "It's true isn't it? That's why you were so surprised when I said that Lucy looked like you."

"Yes," he agreed heavily. "That's why." He spoke slowly, uncertainly, looking suddenly older than his thirty-five years. "My first thought when I found out, was to divorce Laura at once. I think my pride was hurt more than anything else because I certainly didn't care anything for her by then. Anyway, I let her persuade me to take her back—we hadn't been living together as man and wife for months and there was no one else I wanted to marry, so it didn't seem to matter much. When Lucy was born I didn't want anything to do with her . . . for that matter, neither did Laura. She hired Gianetta to look after her and only went near her about once a week. For a couple of months after Laura died I never went near the nursery or Lucy . . . poor little soul. She had no one except Gianetta for all that time." He sighed again, regretfully. "Anyway, one day your mother wrote and asked for a photograph. I went along to look at Lucy and . . . I suddenly realized what a cold blooded bastard I had been to her. It wasn't her fault what had happened. I had agreed to acknowledge her as my daughter yet I certainly hadn't treated her as though she were. I stayed with her for a short while that day and from then on things changed."

He smiled faintly. "I guess you might say I fell in love with her."

He lifted his head from Anne's shoulder and looked closely at her. "Anyway, that's how it is, Anne. I don't know how you feel about it—whether knowing what you know you can still feel the same way about her. But now she *is* my daughter and she'll never be anything else but that."

Anne leaned forward and laid her lips against his cheek. "I love you," she whispered, "and I love Lucy. That's all that matters, isn't it?"

"Oh, Anne!" he groaned and pulled her to him, his mouth tender against her swollen, bruised face. Anne's eyes closed as she felt his lips move softly across her mouth and her cheeks and her eyelids. The horrors of the day receded into merely a nightmare, a not-to-be-forgotten, but no longer frightening, nightmare.

In a little while, with great gentleness he lifted her in his arms and carried her back to the house. Anne now felt dazed and peculiar as delayed shock began to send shivers through her body. She thought she heard Lucy's voice and Tom's, but these sounds were far away and the only real thing was Luke, and his arms warm and close about her. She was gently laid on a bed and covered up with a rug fetched from Luke's car, and she felt his mouth soft on hers before thankfully drifting off to sleep.

You had to admit, Tom thought, that when Luke Patterson moved, he moved quickly. Of course, a rich man had certain resources not open to a man like himself. Still, Luke's riches had not made him soft by any means. Having seen him take that flying rugby tackle to bring Simon to the ground with an almighty thud as Lucy, with Simon in hot pursuit, came charging out of the rhododendron bushes in front of them, he couldn't possibly think he was soft. The rugby tackle had been followed by a fight that was as swift as it was nasty, leaving both men covered in mud, and Simon very much bruised and knocked about. Having checked that his brother was definitely unconscious, Luke spent a few moments soothing and comforting a stricken Lucy before handing her over to Tom and going off to seek Anne.

Now Anne too was safe, and sound asleep on the one bed that looked clean and reasonably well-aired.

"The phone isn't connected," Luke said. "I'll go down to the town to phone through to Giovanni to bring up all the staff. If we're going to stay here for a while we'll need food and blankets and candles. And the place needs cleaning up." He glanced towards the open door of Anne's room. "I'd better get the doctor too."

"What about him?" Tom indicated Simon, who was trussed up like a parcel, Tom having gone to town on him with a large ball of strong thin twine. He was now deposited on a settee, a good deal more comfortable a position than the one he had left Anne in. "The police?"

Luke shook his head. "It's not the police he needs."

"You're not going to try to cover *this* up!" Tom cried incredulously. "I know he's your brother but. . . ."

"Exactly! He's my brother. Look, Tom, let me handle it. You've been a great help so I guess you're entitled to have your say. But I'd rather get Simon back to the States where he can be treated than hand him over to the Italian police."

Tom shrugged. "Okay. You're the boss."

"So keep an eye on things while I'm gone."

"Daddy, let me come with you," Lucy cried. She had been in Luke's arms all this time, her own arms tightly round his neck. He could feel that the fear was in her still, from the stiff urgency of her grasp and the rigidity of her warm little body. She was frightened to death of letting him out of her sight. He kissed her gently.

"It's late, honey. Time you went to bed."

"No!" she sobbed, clinging tighter. "You'll go away again."

"I'll only be gone a little while," he soothed.

"I don't want you to go," Lucy whimpered, genuinely afraid.

The two men's eyes met. "Why don't I go?" Tom suggested. "I know my Italian isn't brilliant but I know how to use a phone. I can get through to Gianetta and tell her what's been happening, then she can see to the doctor and everything."

Luke was easily persuaded. He went outside,

carrying Lucy, and they watched Tom drive off in the Porsche, watching until the rear lights of the car had disappeared into the gloomy evening. Then Luke put Lucy on the big double bed where Anne was sleeping, pulling a rug over both of them. Lucy slept almost at once and Luke, setting the candles so that they would not shine directly into the faces of the sleepers, settled himself down in a chair beside the bed. He would stay there all night if necessary, determined to be there, the first person either of them would see, when they awoke.

ABOUT THE AUTHOR

ANNE NEVILLE lives with her husband in the beautiful cathedral town of Salisbury in Wiltshire, England—and teaches primary school in a small village nearby. She has published ten contemporary romances and also writes historical novels under the name Jane Viney. Her favorite ways of relaxing are horseback riding, dressmaking and embroidery.

CIRCLE OF LOVE

Step out of your world and enter the Circle of Love.

Six new CIRCLE OF LOVE romances are available every month. Here's a preview of the six newest titles, on sale April 15, 1982:

☐ **THE BOTTICELLI MAN** by Alexandra Blakelee (#21515-9 • $1.75)

Young American art student Ursula Stewart stood before Count Enrico Benvoglio in the dazzling Roman sunshine. He opened the door of his chauffeured black Mercedes and whisked her off into the velvet Italian night. His resemblance to a fifteenth-century Botticelli masterpiece was uncanny! But Ursula soon discovered that Enrico was very much a twentieth-century man—and too dangerously seductive for any woman to trust.

☐ **VOICES OF LOVING** by Anne Neville (#21538-8 • $1.75)

Jane Murray fell in love with Max Carstairs the first time she saw the famed actor. But soon tragedy drove Max into a reclusive new identity as a mystery writer. Now, unbelievably, Jane was Max's private secretary, winning his trust, igniting his passion. But she hadn't counted on Margot Copeland, a dazzling, dangerous rival, who would stop at nothing to steal Max's love.

☐ **LOVE'S DREAM** by Christine West (#21514-0 • $1.75)

Sharon's job took her far away from the civilized Australian seacoast to a cattle station in the vast Outback—and to Nat, who tantalized her, yet seemed forever beyond her grasp. Like the land itself, Nat was harsh, overbearing and implacable, challenging Sharon to tame his dauntless spirit and claim her place in his wild heart.

□ **THREAD OF SCARLET** by Rachel Murray
(#21512-4 • $1.75)

Scarlett of Raxby, one of England's finest mills, had chosen Coralie
Dee to design their new mail-order line. Could she possibly succeed
in such a lofty position? And what about Jethro Scarlett himself?
He reassured her one moment only to bully her the next. Yet she felt
bound to this dynamic, darkly handsome man, drawn ever closer by
an invisible, irresistible thread of affection.

□ **HERON'S KEEP** by Samantha Clare (#21513-2 • $1.75)

Jenna had taken the job of secretary to Ross Trent, master of
Heron's Keep, to discover her family's secrets and to reclaim their
rightful place in the ancient Scottish castle. But then, Jenna became
torn by yearning for this man she couldn't afford to possess. How
long could she walk the tightrope between desire and deceit until
Ross finally discovered the truth?

□ **MIDSUMMER DREAMS** by Amalia James
(#21511-6 • $1.75)

When Maxine's grandparents asked her to help them run their
beautiful inn in the Berkshires, she finally decided to put her fading
dreams of a glittering Broadway career behind her. But then Carter
Richardson, a brilliant director, rented the inn for the summer—and
Max knew that the theater was in her blood. And Carter was never
out of her thoughts. But how could Maxine ever compete with
Carter's leading lady for fame and love?

_____

_____

BANTAM BOOKS, INC. Dept. CR, 414 East Golf Road,
Des Plaines, IL 60016

Please send me the books I have checked above. I am enclosing
$_____ (please add $1.00 to cover postage and
handling). Send check or money order—no cash or C.O.D.'s
please.

Mr/Mrs/Miss_____

Address_____

City_____ State/Zip_____

CR-4/82

Please allow four to six weeks for delivery.
This offer expires 10/82.

SAVE $2.00 ON YOUR NEXT BOOK ORDER!

BANTAM BOOKS ✦
Shop-at-Home —
Catalog

Now you can have a complete, up-to-date catalog of Bantam's inventory of over 1,600 titles—including hard-to-find books.

And, you can save $2.00 on your next order by taking advantage of the money–saving coupon you'll find in this illustrated catalog. Choose from fiction and non-fiction titles, including mysteries, historical novels, westerns, cookbooks, romances, biographies, family living, health, and more. You'll find a description of most titles. Arranged by categories, the catalog makes it easy to find your favorite books and authors and to discover new ones.

So don't delay—send for this shop-at-home catalog and save money on your next book order.

Just send us your name and address and 50¢ to defray postage and handling costs.

- -

BANTAM BOOKS, INC.
Dept. FC, 414 East Golf Road, Des Plaines, Ill. 60016

Mr./Mrs./Miss_____
(please print)
Address_____

City_____State_____Zip_____

Do you know someone who enjoys books? Just give us their names and addresses and we'll send them a catalog too at no extra cost!

_____

Mr./Mrs./Miss_____

Address_____

City_____State_____Zip_____

_____

Mr./Mrs./Miss_____

Address_____

City_____State_____Zip_____

FC—9/81